WHERE OUR HEARTS LIE

TRINITY LAKES ROMANCE BOOK SIX

JENNY GLAZEBROOK

CHAPTER ONE

Why couldn't she stop shaking? Hallie took a deep breath and blew it out slowly. She rubbed clammy hands down her skirt. She was doing this. She was really doing this. Two years of internet dating, and tonight she was meeting Dave Holden in person for the first time. Hard to believe he had relatives here in Springfield. If only she'd admitted where she lived from the very start. But life had taught her to be cautious. And what were the chances that someone who lived in Miami had relatives in Springfield, Missouri?

She glanced around the crowded restaurant. Soft music played and couples chatted over their meals. One family entertained their tousle-haired toddler and laughed at something he said.

Such a warm, friendly atmosphere. Perhaps Amanda had been right suggesting this was the best meeting place. Not because the park wasn't safe if Dave pulled a gun on her—Amanda was so dramatic, thinking the worst of every situation—but because this was what Hallie had always dreamed of. Meeting her future husband in a romantic place like this, falling in love, perhaps even experiencing her first kiss.

She'd chosen a secluded section of the restaurant. After all, Dave was hard of hearing—a result of too many ear infections in his younger surfing years. He could lip-read, but she was sure a quieter environment would be best.

"Hallie, you waiting for someone?" A waitress gave a tight smile on her way past, dirty dishes balanced skillfully in her hands.

Hallie tensed. Simone. Of all people, why did Simone have to be working here tonight?

Simone stopped and retraced her steps, eyes widening. "No, don't tell me. You're on a date?"

The disbelief in her eyes irked Hallie. Was it really so hard to believe someone would date her? To be fair, she supposed it was. What other woman had her first date at the age of twenty-one? The truth was, Hallie had never had a boyfriend. From her teen years, when no one wanted to date the "genius missionary kid," right through into her adulthood, she had never fit in. But finally, finally someone knew all about her and wanted to meet her.

She smiled sweetly at Simone. "Yes, I'm meeting someone."

Simone darted a glance around the restaurant. "Where is he?"

"I'm early."

Simone smirked. The same smirk she'd given Hallie in Sunday School all those years ago when the teacher asked her to let the other children have a chance to answer the questions. It wasn't that Hallie was rude or interrupting. It was just that the other children weren't answering. And Hallie knew the answers like any missionary kid should.

"Well ..." Simone drew the word out. "Have a good night then."

"Thank you." Hallie tried not to grit her teeth as Simone sashayed back to the kitchen. Okay, so Amanda's idea to meet Dave here hadn't been such a good idea.

Her phone pinged. She smiled at the image of Dave on his surfboard. It embodied who he was. A guy from Florida, soaking up the surf and sand God had made for him to enjoy.

She read his text.

So sorry, my car broke down.

Her fingers danced across her phone screen. *Are you okay? Where are you?*

His answer came back quickly. *Claydon Park.*

Only a few blocks away. The place she'd originally wanted to meet him. Away from Simone. Maybe this was a sign from God.

She texted back. *I'll get to-go bags and meet you there. What would you like?*

You choose.

She smiled. The fish and chips would work. A typical Florida surfer, he must surely love all things connected with the ocean.

She moved to the counter. Simone came to the register.

"Everything okay?"

Hallie stood taller. "Yes. His car broke down. Can we get to-go bags?"

One of Simone's eyebrows lifted, doubt written all over her face. Hallie stared her down.

After what seemed like another ice age, Simone focused on the register. "So what can I get you?"

"Fish and chips. For two."

Now both Simone's brows lifted. "For a date?"

"Dave's a surfer." Hallie snapped her mouth closed. Why had she said Dave's name? She didn't need to defend her decision, and she definitely didn't want to share any of tonight with Simone.

"So he's probably sick of fish and chips." Simone pointed to the specials board. "The grilled deluxe is good."

Of all the …

"No, thank you. Two orders of fish and chips, please. Finger food is easier while waiting for roadside assistance."

Simone blinked as though nobody had dared defy her before. Her fingers tapped heavily on the register buttons.

"Fish and chips it is." Her tone said exactly what she thought of the order.

Hallie refused to doubt herself. Tonight wasn't about the food. It was about meeting her best friend for the first time. The friend who'd taken the loneliness from her evenings, who'd made her feel special and valued. It didn't matter that they'd never met in person before. It was the heart that mattered. And Dave's heart was good. She knew it with everything within her.

She sat in the waiting chairs and pulled out her phone.

I've ordered. Be there soon.

He sent back a smiley face. *Can't wait.*

She tried not to jiggle. She was normally self-controlled, displaying all the fruit of the Spirit and checking them off in order, but tonight patience was hard to find. So was peace.

Lord, please help me. Please let tonight go well.

She knew God had heard and he cared. His plans for her were good.

The chef came out holding two bags. "Hallie Hollaway?"

Finally.

With a quick thank you, Hallie made her escape.

She shot Dave another text. *On my way.*

Juggling her keys in one hand and her purse and to-go bags in the other, she unlocked her car. *Lord, please help me be calm. Settle my heart.*

She glanced at herself in the rearview mirror. Nothing could be done about flyaway red hair and freckles, but should she put some more makeup on? No, Dave was a surfer. He would be used to sun-kissed skin and the natural outdoor look.

She shot Dave another text. *Which side of the park are you on?*

She waited.

I'm at the water fountain.

. . .

HALLIE'S HEART pounded harder as she pulled into the parking lot. There were very few cars here this time of night. All had Missouri plates apart from one, a silver Honda Accord with Indiana plates. That wasn't likely to be Dave. She got out and wiped her hands down her skirt. This summer heat wasn't mixing well with her nerves. It was a warm evening and she regretted not buying drinks to go with their meal.

She walked on the grass to avoid her heels making noise on the sidewalk.

The smell of fish and chips wafted up, but she didn't think she could eat, not with the way her stomach churned with nerves. She drew in another deep breath. Dave said he loved *her*, not her appearance. He loved who she was deep down inside. The person he'd come to know through her emails and phone calls. He loved her faith and her heart for God. She had to believe that.

"Hallie?"

She heard him before she saw him. His voice was deep. Warm.

"Dave?"

She stepped into the light from the fountain and Dave beamed at her. Except it wasn't Dave. It was an older man. Balding, gray, and slightly paunchy. Definitely no bleach-blond hair and tanned surfer body.

"Hallie." The man said her name as though he knew her. "You're waiting for Dave."

She took a step back. "I am. Who are you?"

What was happening here? Had this man done something to Dave? Or did he bring one of his relatives with him?

"I'm his friend."

A balding man around sixty? He didn't look like the kind of friend she'd expect surfer Dave to have. But who was she to judge? She kept her voice calm.

"Oh. Where's Dave?"

He pointed the opposite direction. "The roadside assist team arrived. He asked me to wait here with you."

Hallie smiled, but she couldn't let down her guard. Something wasn't adding up. "That was quick." She scanned the area. Where was Dave's car? She could see a couple of cars across the other side of the park, but she couldn't make them out clearly from this far away. A large tree blocked her view. Perhaps Dave's car and the roadside assist team were hidden by it. She glanced back at Dave's friend. He was studying her too intently. She looked away.

"So ... um ..."

"You're just like your picture," he said.

"My picture?"

"Yes. Red hair. Freckles. So young."

Dave had showed him her picture?

He tilted his head to the side and squinted at her. "You're not really twenty-one and working in a library, are you?"

Her heart stuttered. How did he know her age or where she worked? She wasn't comfortable with this man, Dave's friend or not. She took a step back.

"What did Dave tell you about me?"

The man smiled. "Everything. He told me how beautiful you are. And he was right." He stepped closer. Touched her hand.

Was he hitting on her? How dare he? She pulled back further. She just wanted to see Dave. But why had he told this man about her? Disquiet made its way from her heart to her head. She'd thought she could trust Dave. Something wasn't right.

"I'd like to see Dave now, please." Her voice shook. Was it fear, or anger because this stranger was acting as though he knew her? She wasn't sure.

He smiled. "He'll be here soon." Still, his gaze pinned her down, too familiar, too intense. "He sent a message for you."

Hallie lifted her phone to look. The man pushed her hand down.

"No, not a text. He asked me to give you the message."

Hallie darted a glance around the park. Did she need to run? What about Dave? She'd been waiting so long to meet him. But she'd be telling him exactly what she thought of his friend.

The man blinked slowly. "The message from Dave is that he knows what's in your heart. You love him and he loves you. It doesn't matter what you look like, what lies you might have told, any ways you may have exaggerated the truth. It's about what's in your heart."

What was he saying? Anger and indignation overcame any fear.

"I did not tell any lies. I am twenty-one and everything I told Dave is true. How dare you assume I've lied to him?"

The man chuckled. "Love makes us do crazy things, doesn't it?"

What was he talking about? This guy was crazy. She took another step back, and another. He stalked her, step for step. She stopped and grabbed her phone, punched the button to call Dave.

"No," the man said. "Don't …"

A phone rang. In his back pocket. He automatically reached for it, then stopped. It continued ringing. Hallie pressed her phone to her ear, watching the man's every move.

Come on Dave, pick up. Please God, let him pick up.

It rang out. The man's phone fell silent.

Hallie stared. Her hands shook. "Who are you?"

"I'm Dave," he said. "Although my real name is Malcolm. Everything else is true. Everything I sent you in those emails, everything I wrote, that's the real me. And I love you."

No. It couldn't be.

And yet she knew it was.

She simultaneously kicked off her heels, dropped the bag of fish and chips, and ran.

Amanda had been right. She was too trusting. Simone had been right. No man would genuinely fall in love with a red-headed genius misfit. No man except a crazy, lying stalker. Being desperate for love made you believe crazy things.

CHAPTER TWO

Josh Ladan wandered into the Bellbird Café. His friend Brandon Taylor was already there, lounging back, sipping from a can of soda. Typical Brandon. Acting as though this fancy café was a diner to lounge in. Brandon spotted him and lifted his hand in a wave.

Josh wanted to laugh. If Brandon was trying to be inconspicuous, he was doing a poor job of it. His jeans were streaked with grease, and his thick, dark hair poked up in all directions.

Josh slid into the seat across from him and grinned. "Didn't bother to change after work?"

Brandon chuckled. "Look who's talking."

Josh glanced down at his cotton work shirt with the "Lakes Fresh Food Store" logo on the pocket. "Yeah, but my job isn't dirty like yours."

"Because you don't have a real job."

Josh rolled his eyes, used to his friend's teasing. Maybe stacking supermarket shelves wasn't a career in some people's estimation, but Josh didn't like to push himself. He'd done that a few years ago. Learned his lesson. He subconsciously rubbed the spot at the back of his head where the migraines still came.

One head injury during a visit to Australia to see his grandparents, and all his dreams had come crashing down. But life was good. He had plenty of friends, enough money to do whatever he wanted to do—which wasn't much—and he lived in the most beautiful place in the world. Trinity Lakes was a taste of heaven.

Brandon fiddled with the ring pull on his can of soda. "Jodie working tonight?"

Josh studied him. Brandon seemed to be asking about Jodie's whereabouts an awful lot lately. Surely he wasn't interested in his sister? Jodie was such a hopeless romantic and Brandon was … not. Not likely she'd be happy married to an auto mechanic when she'd always dreamed of going to college and "getting a real job" as a journalist.

Josh didn't mind people poking fun at him about his job. He asked for it, the way he kept pointing out that he wasn't stressed. He wasn't rushing around trying to complete assignments and please professors. No, his brain injury had been a blessing in disguise. He now understood it wasn't worth pushing for anything. You couldn't control your life so you might as well sit back and go with the flow. He was determined to be happily relaxed. And happily single.

"Don't even think about her, Brando," he said.

Brandon dropped the ring pull. "What?"

"Jodie. She's high maintenance. Not worth it."

Brandon snorted. "Who said I'm interested in her that way? But if I was—and I'm saying if—you wouldn't understand. You're her brother."

"And you're my friend, so I'm helping you by warning you what you'd be getting yourself into."

Brandon threw the ring pull at Josh. Josh laughed as he caught it neatly and dropped it onto the table. Then he stiffened.

"Look out. Here she comes." He said the words out the side

of his mouth and Brandon glanced around. Then slid lower into his seat.

Kyla. She had a thing for Brandon. Or was it him? Josh wasn't sure, but she'd been on the prowl ever since she'd broken up with her fiancé. It was crazy. She was too old for them. She must be close to thirty.

It was no use hiding. Her sharp gaze landed on them, and her mouth broke into a wide smile.

"Joshua. Brandon. What are you doing here?"

Josh swapped a look with Brandon. What would happen if they told her the truth? That Brandon was bored with Joe's Diner and had challenged him to try a new place? Brandon was good like that, making sure he didn't become too comfortable in his own world. If he was honest, he would never try anything new if it weren't for Brandon.

"Mind if I join you?" She didn't wait for an answer. She slid into the seat beside Josh. He was trapped. How were they going to get out of this one?

Brandon's phone buzzed. He pulled it from his pocket, frowned at the screen then jumped up. He glanced at Josh, his expression urgent. "I gotta go."

Confused, Josh watched the café door swish closed behind him as he charged outside. What had just happened? It wasn't like Brandon to bail on him. And the plan had been for Brandon to drive him home.

He typed a quick text.

U ok? Surely he wasn't doing this to test him? Brandon was the one he could trust. The friend who always had his back.

Kyla was saying something, trying to get his attention. He turned to face her. Tried to listen.

"So." She beamed at him like a cat who had the cream. "What were you going to have?" She opened the menu, and he drew in a deep breath. She'd better not expect him to read it. She was the last person he'd want to discover he couldn't. Alexia was not a condition he was proud of, or something he talked about. Only his closest friend and family knew what the concussion had done to him that summer break in Australia. Brain injuries were complex, the neurosurgeon had said. And this one was permanent. All those years at school learning to read had been a waste. He fiddled with the corner of the menu Kyla had placed in front of him. If he'd been at Joe's Diner, he would at least know what was on the menu.

He cleared his throat and met Kyla's dark eyes. "Ah ... I actually only came to see Brandon. I wasn't planning on staying."

"Come on. My treat." She looked at him as though there was no way he could say no. And he found he couldn't bring himself to hurt her feelings.

"Just a Coke for me," he mumbled, glancing desperately around. He needed an escape. Needed to know if Brandon was okay.

"I saw you at church on Sunday but didn't get a chance to say hello." Kyla tilted her head at him. "When will we see you preaching?"

He tried not to wince. Never. He'd once dreamed of being a preacher like his father. Had even earned a baseball scholarship to Grace Seminary before his accident. Being a pastor obviously wasn't God's plan for him.

Thankfully Kyla was distracted by a waitress passing by. She lifted her hand. The waitress walked right past.

Kyla snapped her fingers. "Excuse me."

The waitress turned back, and Josh studied the tablecloth. Just sitting with Kyla was enough to tarnish his reputation. Everyone knew the girl wanted a husband. He wasn't sure of the full story, but she'd almost caught one of the Kennedys. It had been a lucky escape according to Brandon. He'd heard someone talking about how the breakup had triggered something in her. Changed her. Rumor said their pastor didn't insist Caleb marry her, so she'd changed churches. Now she was trying out their church. Lucky them.

Kyla was speaking to the waitress.

"Josh will have a Coke," she said, "and a chocolate muffin." She shot a smug glance at him. "I know you like chocolate muffins. I saw you having one during refreshments."

What? Oh, coffee break at church. She was watching him?

"I love your Australian accent," she said. "Did you get that from your mom, or from your year of vacationing in Australia?"

She knew about his time in Australia? It definitely couldn't be described as a vacation despite him pretending to all those who knew him that it was. His week-long visit to his grandparents had turned into a year in the hospital and rehab.

Kyla smiled at him. "I've noticed your accent is a bit different, though. Not fully Australian, is it? Or do they have different dialects over there?"

Josh blinked. It was called having a traumatic brain injury—TBI—and having to learn to speak again. Yes, his accent was influenced by the Australians caring for him and growing up with an Australian mother, but Kyla was the first one who'd questioned it. She was too close to the truth. Too observant. This called for emergency measures.

"I guess they have different dialects," he said. He stood. "Excuse me. I'm just heading to the men's room."

She smiled and moved aside to let him out.

The moment he rounded the corner into the men's room, he pulled out his phone. Brandon hadn't answered his text. He tried ringing him. Nothing. He called his sister instead.

Jodie picked up straight away. "Josh?"

"Jodes, quick, I need your help. I'm stuck here in the Bellbird with Kyla. Brandon bailed."

"With Kyla?" Jodie's voice held concern. She knew Kyla. Had been the recipient of her dark looks and snide comments at church these past few weeks.

"I'm on my way down." Jodie's voice hardened. "And I'll drag Brandon back there too. What kind of friend does that?"

Josh would have laughed if he wasn't so concerned. There was Jodie, always ready to do battle on his behalf. Guilt niggled. He'd told Brandon she was high maintenance, but that was an exaggeration.

"I'm sure he had a good reason."

"He'd better have. I'll be there in a few minutes."

Josh ended the call and peeked around the corner. Kyla was tapping her fingers on the table. He sighed and forced himself to join her. This time he sat opposite.

She gave him a bright smile. "I hear your sister wants to be a journalist." She gave a little laugh as though it was a ridiculous notion.

Josh gritted his teeth. "She does. And she's quite capable."

"But isn't she working as a receptionist?"

She didn't say it, but he heard the "just" in there. "Yes. At the Bible College. It's an involved job. She's working there while she saves up to go to Columbia. She's pretty bright."

"Oh?" Kyla looked doubtful. "What was her GPA?"

"I don't know." It was true. He hadn't bothered to ask. "But I'm sure she did well." Just as he had. But what use had good grades been when he'd lost the ability to read only months later?

Kyla blinked. "I would've thought she'd want to be in some kind of full-time ministry. Journalism's not a Christian scene."

Josh smirked. "Jodie likes to ferret out the truth. She tells it like it is. Truth is very important to Christians, don't you think?"

Kyla sat up straighter. "That's what people say about me. So many Christians like to sugarcoat the truth. They water down the Word of God. God calls us to stand for Him. When I was in …"

Josh zoned out her story about how she'd helped the Book Club by pointing out the books they read weren't really Christian. It was all Josh could do not to roll his eyes. He definitely owed Jodie an apology for saying she was high maintenance. Or at least he needed to rescind what he'd said to Brandon. Compared with Kyla, Jodie was a saint.

The door burst open and everybody jumped, spinning to face the door. Jodie rushed in.

"Josh! Quick, I need to talk to you."

He tried not to laugh. What a champion. She was a brilliant actress. Her golden hair was falling from her high ponytail, her face was pale, and her hands were … they were shaking.

He jumped up. "Jodie?"

She had already rushed back outside. Josh's heart pounded. He didn't even glance back at Kyla as he raced out the door. Jodie was already in her car. Her hands were on the steering wheel, ready to go. Her words ran together. "I saw an ambulance outside Brandon's place. The paramedics were unloading a stretcher."

Josh tried to process the information.

Jodie's voice shook. "Quick. Get in."

He jumped in and she screeched the tires and took off before he had a chance to buckle up his seatbelt. If the situation hadn't been so serious, he'd tease her about it. She was the one always calling out Brandon for his reckless driving.

Josh and Jodie arrived to find Brandon's mother sitting on the front steps of her house talking with the paramedics. It looked like she was arguing. Brandon stood beside her.

Jodie reached them first. "Everything okay?"

Brandon rubbed a hand through his hair, messing it up further. "Mom had a turn. She collapsed."

"Pfft." His mother shook her head. "It was a dizzy spell is all. It's this summer heat. I got dehydrated, okay? I'll drink some more now."

One of the paramedics touched her arm. "We'd like you to come to the hospital for some tests just the same." It was Jocelyn, from church.

Brandon's mother glowered. "I can come to the hospital for tests on my own. I'm not hopping into that ambulance like a drama queen and being ferried to the hospital for a little dizzy spell."

"Mom ..."

"Brandon, stop fussing. I'm fine."

But even Josh could see she wasn't.

"What if Brandon takes you in?" Jodie asked. Good old Jodes. Always the peacemaker.

Brandon's mother frowned. "He just got home from work."

Brandon's arm went around her shoulders. "As if I care about that, Mom. I'll take you. Please."

She sighed and her shoulders dropped. "Fine. If you must."

Jocelyn held out a clipboard with a form. "Mrs. Taylor, we just need you to sign to say you declined transport with us to the hospital."

"Ms.," Brandon's mother hissed. "It's Ms. Taylor."

Josh met Jodie's eye and they smiled. Brandon's mom could be a battle-ax, but Brandon loved her with complete devotion. If he'd treat his own wife with such care someday, then perhaps Jodie wouldn't be a fool to respond to Brandon's interest rather than chasing her dreams.

Josh looked at Brandon. "Want us to come?"

Brandon shook his head. "Nah, we'll be right. Come on, Mom."

"So bossy." Ms. Taylor glared at her son, but there was also affection in her eyes as she allowed him to lead her to the car.

CHAPTER THREE

Was she doing the right thing? Hallie sniffled as Amanda handed her a box of tissues and settled her on her sofa with an iced coffee. Amanda's motherly care was just what she needed.

"You have to report him, Hallie."

Hallie rubbed her eyes. "For what? For pretending to be someone he isn't?"

"Yes. He's a con artist."

Hallie bit her lip, swiping at more tears. "No, I'm a fool."

"Stop it." Amanda put both hands on Hallie's shoulders and waited until Hallie lifted her eyes. "You're the smartest girl I know. Being trusting doesn't make you a fool. It makes you someone who wants to believe in people. Who gives them a chance."

Hallie stared down at her bare feet now dirty from her dash through the park. "Because I was desperate. That's my whole problem, Amanda. I'm so desperate for love that I grasped at the first person who showed any interest in me. A person I'd never even met."

"Hallie." Amanda's voice was gentle now. "You are worthy of

love. Not because you're an amazing person, which you are, but because God loves you. He made you. You know this. You're a missionary kid. As an MK, you've heard about the love of Jesus your whole life. You don't need to do anything special to be loved by Jesus. You just are."

Hallie knew it was true. "But …"

"But what, Hallie? What holds you back from making friends? From letting anyone close?"

Hallie looked up into Amanda's eyes, hurt. "I let people close. I let you close."

Amanda shook her head. "Because I'm your boss." A smile tilted her lips. "You have to like me, or life would be miserable." Amanda shifted on the sofa. "I'm your mother's age, Hallie. Why do you seek friendship and approval from older people?"

It was a good question.

"Because I miss my parents?"

Amanda sat back. "I don't think so."

Hallie blinked. "Pardon?"

"Hallie, you told me you finished your homeschooling as soon as you could so your parents could go back to the mission field. That doesn't sound like a daughter who misses her parents."

Hallie blinked harder.

Amanda stood, pulled Hallie up from the sofa and wrapped her in a hug. "I think you should stay here tonight. I'll drop you home to pack an overnight bag, then I'll bring you right back here."

Hallie was shaken enough that she agreed.

"Ray, I'm taking Hallie home to grab some things," Amanda called to her husband.

"Sure," Ray called from down the hall. "I'll make the spare bed."

Hallie let a smile peek through. Amanda and Ray were true friends, and she loved the way they worked as a team. Their marriage was filled with love and understanding. Her breath hitched. She might never have that. It seemed she only attracted scam artists. Or was he a psycho? Either way … But what did "Dave" really want?

Her phone tinged as though he'd heard her thoughts. She shivered as she read his message.

Please give me a chance. I know you love me as much as I love you. We can make this work.

"From him?" Amanda started up the car and pulled out of her garage.

Hallie pulled her seatbelt across and clicked it into place. "Yep."

Another text came. *You'll regret it if you walk away from what we have. We need to talk. Meet me in the park in half an hour.*

Now that was just plain demanding. Was it also a veiled threat? Hallie didn't know what to think. She grieved for the loss of Dave, yet he'd never existed. She was grieving her dream.

Amanda rounded the corner into Hallie's street when Hallie spotted it. A silver Honda Accord with Indiana plates outside her house. The same one she'd seen at the park.

Her hand flew out to grip Amanda's arm.

"Manda! I think that's him." She pointed a shaking finger at the car. Amanda slowed, then turned into the closest street.

"You're not going home tonight, Hallie. We're going to the police."

Hallie didn't argue.

HALLIE TRIED to stop her hands shaking as she was taken into an interview room with a detective. She was glad to have Amanda with her. Detective Cole took her phone to go through her texts and emails while some other officers went out in search of Dave.

"We're sorry to do this," Detective Cole said after he'd made some calls. "We have our suspicions about his identity. If we're right, he's a convicted pedophile on parole. The car license plate you gave us is from a stolen car. Is there anywhere you can go for the time being? Any family or friends in another state?"

Hallie bit her lip. "No." Amanda was her only friend. Apart from … her mind traveled back to her childhood years. The Ladan family.

"I could go to Trinity Lakes."

"Where?" Amanda's face pinched.

"Trinity Lakes. In Washington. Where my parents went to Bible college. I've always wanted to go back." It was the only place she'd ever been happy. The only place she felt like she belonged.

The police officer tapped something into his computer then turned with a smile. "That should work. It's close to two thousand miles away. I can contact the county Sheriff there. You'll need to make sure you make yourself known to them as soon as you arrive."

Amanda frowned. "She can't drive all that way on her own."

"I agree." The detective gave Amanda a reassuring smile. "It would be safest to fly—put as many miles between herself and Springfield as quickly as possible. Just until we find him." He looked at Hallie. "Is there somewhere safe you can stay tonight? Some officers can then accompany you to pack tomorrow morning."

"She's staying at my place."

The officer nodded at Amanda. "Sounds like a plan. We'll have officers patrolling the area tonight, but my guess is he's been tipped off and is on the run."

"Knock, knock." Amanda knocked on the door frame to the spare room.

Hallie looked up and smiled. "Come in." She felt much better after a shower, although Amanda's pajamas were too short for her.

"You doing okay?"

Hallie nodded. "I did a lot of thinking and praying in the shower. I'm wondering if this is all part of God's plan—His way of moving me on from Springfield."

Amanda's eyes widened as Hallie's words sank in. "You want to move to Trinity Lakes? Permanently? But Hallie, your job, your life here ..."

"If I move out of Mom and Dad's house, they can rent it out. The money will help with their mission work."

"You can't sacrifice your calling for your parent's calling, Hallie. That's not what God asks us to do."

Hallie turned away. "What if my calling isn't here, Amanda? I enjoy the library, but I feel there's something more for me."

"But you were made for the library. The kids who come in love you. You're so passionate about stories. I've never known anyone like you. No one else I know finished homeschool and completed a Bachelor in Library and Information Science as young as you did."

"And that's why I'm a misfit here." Hallie sighed. "I'm tired of being the MK genius, Amanda. I want a fresh start. Away from here. With people who knew me before ..."

"Before what?"

Hallie turned away. "Just before."

Amanda sighed. "Well, you've got a lot of vacation owing. Why don't you go visit first, until they catch Malcolm ... and think and pray more about it while you're there?"

Hallie nodded, already picturing the beautiful lakes and mountains around Trinity Lakes. The faces of friends who understood her. Other children who had been missionary kids and pastor's kids. Excitement mixed with nervous energy.

Lord, please protect and guide me.

. . .

HALLIE JERKED AWAKE, drenched in sweat. The nightmare was back. Only this time it hadn't been the rebels on the island threatening her. It was Malcolm.

She covered her eyes, replaying the trauma of her childhood, unable to make it stop, though she had vowed it would never hold any power over her again. She fixed her eyes on the wall of Ray and Amanda's guest bedroom as the memories took hold.

Her mother's sweet face contorted in anger and fear while her father stood poised, machete in hand.

She, ten years old, huddled in the corner, waiting, wondering if she was about to die. Her mother's voice called out through the darkness.

"John, you have to get her out of here. This is not the place for a child! I told you she doesn't belong here."

Hallie had been too terrified to think on her mother's words at the time, but they had plagued her ever since.

"Quick, Hallie, under the bed," her father's voice was raspy, and Hallie knew he was afraid too.

The voices outside became louder as the angry islanders banged on the door, shouting demands and cursing the missionaries. It didn't take much to break down the flimsy door and find the girl still too terrified to hide.

Hallie screamed and fought against the arms that held her. "Let me go!"

The hold around her neck tightened, and she gasped for breath. Her father stepped forward, his expression resolute.

"What do you want?"

"We want you out of our land. Go home."

Hallie watched the unspoken message pass between her parents. Would they agree? Their whole lives had been built around these people—reaching them, loving them, sharing the Gospel. Three years at Trinity Lakes Bible College and another year of cultural training, and now this group of rebels had taken exception to what they believed was political interference. She watched as her father sighed and his shoulders slumped in defeat.

"Give us a week, and we'll be gone."

If Hallie thought returning to the US would make her world secure again, her first day back at school had proved her wrong.

"Look at her hair. It's so red."

"Why do you talk like a grown-up?"

"Are you a genius?"

"You're too young to be in our class."

It took two weeks for her parents to withdraw her from school and continue homeschooling. All the while, Hallie knew she didn't belong. She didn't belong on the island, and she didn't belong in Springfield. She didn't belong in school, and she didn't belong with her parents. She heard her mom crying at night and knew she was the reason they couldn't continue their dream of being missionaries. She hated holding them back, so she'd worked hard at her studies, knowing the sooner she finished and left home, the sooner her parents could return to their beloved island—without the inconvenience and burden of a child.

Now she was no longer a child and she still didn't belong. There was only one place she'd ever felt loved and at home. Trinity Lakes, where being a Christian or the child of missionaries wasn't unusual. The Ladan family had loved her. Had treated her like family. Josh and Jodie had been her friends. They were the only friends she'd ever had around her own age. It was time to go back to Trinity Lakes.

CHAPTER FOUR

Josh lounged in the back row, watching people file into church. Taking the back pew had several advantages. One, he could slip out unnoticed if a migraine hit. Two, no one would notice that he never followed along in the Bible or read the notes on the screen up the front as his father spoke. And three, he could keep an eye out for those who were struggling. Lakes Fresh Food allowed him to take food nearing its use-by date and deliver it to locals in need. It was a job he enjoyed. It made him feel as though he was doing something meaningful with his life.

The final thing he liked about sitting up the back was that he and Brandon could watch everyone as they filed in and store up intel to discuss later. It made church more interesting—noticing peoples' quirks, hearing things he probably shouldn't be hearing. It had become a bit of a game he and Brandon played.

Mrs. Sellers was looking thin as she shuffled into church. Maybe she wasn't eating properly. A few groceries might help.

Brandon nudged him and nodded toward the door. "Incoming."

Josh followed his gaze. Kyla. He ducked his head. Surely she wouldn't sit with them? No, thankfully. Kyla wanted to be noticed. She charged down the front and settled in beside Jodie. Poor Jodie.

Brandon gave an exaggerated swipe of his brow. "Phew. That was close."

Josh chuckled. "She didn't even look this way."

Brandon grinned. "No, but wait until coffee break. She'll be stalking you, taking notes on everything you eat ..."

Josh rolled his eyes. He should have known better than to tell Brandon about Kyla's creepy comments in the café.

The music began and everyone settled into their seats. Josh glanced at old Mr. Carrigan, guarding the church entry as usual.

"Should I offer to take over?" Brandon asked with a boyish, cheeky grin. He was such a stirrer, acting more like a teenager than the twenty-two-year-old man he was. They both knew that asking Mr. Carrigan to step down from his place at the door would cause more trouble than it was worth.

The music began and the first song was announced. Josh stood, then turned when movement at the door caught his eye. A tall young woman walked in. A visitor.

But there was something familiar about the small smile she gave Mr. Carrigan as she accepted the weekly church bulletin. She turned and he saw her bright blue eyes.

A gasp from the front of the church drew their attention. Mom had turned and was looking at the visitor, eyes alight with joy. Then she charged down the aisle.

"Hallie? Hallie is that you?"

The visitor's face lit with recognition. "Aunty Lil?"

No. Josh's heart did a funny leap. That woman wasn't a grown up Hallie Hollaway, was it? She had the red hair, even the freckles, but she was so tall and willowy, with gentle curves that definitely hadn't been there when she was a little girl.

Mom threw her arms around the newcomer and drew her

outside. Even above the music, Josh could hear Mom's excited voice.

Brandon leaned over. "Who is she?" he mouthed.

"An old family friend, I think."

But if it was Hallie, what was she doing here? She was so tall, so grown up. Which made sense considering she'd been ten years old the last time he'd seen her. He shouldn't be disappointed, but he'd liked the little freckled, red-headed girl from his childhood. He'd liked making her smile. Making her laugh had been better than a home run.

The song ended and Mom and the visitor slipped back into church. Josh recognized the walk. Confident. Poised. Yes, it was Hallie.

They slid into an empty row midway down the aisle. Josh didn't hear another word of the service. His mind was filled with memories. Memories of the bright seven-year-old girl who had arrived with her parents at the Bible college. He was a year older, and she'd followed him around and helped him practice baseball. She'd pitched to him over and over again, never seeming to tire of it. Then she allowed him to pitch to her, patiently waiting as he practiced his aim. She'd been the brightest, most caring little girl he'd ever known in the three years she'd been in Trinity Lakes. It was as though she'd been able to see into his heart and cared enough about him to take an interest in his dreams to share his excitement and help him achieve them.

Dreams that had been crushed.

He was vaguely aware of the worship leader announcing refreshments and closing the service with a blessing. He wasn't ready to face Hallie or to tell Brandon who she was. He escaped the church building and moved into the hall before the final amen.

The truth was, he was rattled and he didn't like to be rattled. Hallie looked … like a stranger yet so familiar. He needed to get his bearings before he faced her. He didn't quite know how to reconcile his childhood, brotherly care for the little girl with this tug—of attraction?—he felt for the young woman she'd become.

Thankfully Mrs. Carrigan was already in the hall setting out coffee cups.

She smiled at him. "Josh, can you grab the milk out of the fridge?"

"Sure." Anything to be occupied and delay the inevitable. He set out the milk as people trickled into the room. Then he wiped down the bench though it didn't need it.

He peeked through the service counter window. Brandon leaned against the wall, looking bored as he bit into a donut from the refreshments table. Mom and Jodie came in, Hallie by their side. Jodie was beaming at her long-lost friend. Josh smiled at the memory of seven-year-old Hallie playing Barbies with four-year-old Jodie. She'd played with her right up until she'd left at the age of ten. Hallie had been a good sport. Where had the years gone?

He watched as Jodie dragged Hallie toward Brandon.

"Hallie, this is Brandon. Brandon, meet Hallie."

Brandon stopped just long enough to wipe crumbs from his mouth and give Hallie a polite nod. He chewed until his mouth was empty enough to speak. "Hi."

What would Brandon think of Hallie? Josh knew him well enough to know he would be judging her, looking for any faults, any quirks, anything to put her in her place. Until now, Josh had been happy to be one of the few people in the world Brandon actually liked and approved of. Now he wanted Hallie to be included in that small circle. Judging by Brandon's expression, it wasn't likely to happen.

Hallie's smile was reserved. Was she put off by Brandon's bad manners or his smug, amused expression? She wasn't to know Brandon always had that look on his face—the one that made him appear as though he were privately laughing at you. Which he probably was.

"Hallie's a family friend from way back," Jodie told Brandon. "Her family studied at the Bible college here before they went to the mission field. We haven't seen her for at least ten years, and she wasn't sure we'd still be here. But here we are."

Brandon looked at Hallie. "You thought they might have moved on, hey?" There was something cynical in his smile.

Hallie's blue eyes met his, challenging his skepticism. "It was a distinct possibility. We haven't been in touch for years." Her voice was cultured and confident but sweet.

"And yet your parents' latest missionary photo is on their fridge."

Wow. Brandon was more observant than Josh gave him credit for.

Brandon reached for another donut. "There's an old one with you in it, too. When you were a little kid." He shoved the rest of the donut into his mouth.

Josh saw the disgusted look Jodie gave Brandon and chuckled. Brandon never bothered trying to impress anyone. But Brandon didn't know Hallie. He didn't know how intelligent she was. Didn't know what she'd been through. Didn't know how her little-girl cries had broken Josh's heart.

He slipped out the back door. He needed to pull himself together. Hallie was a grown woman now. She didn't need his sympathy. Didn't need him.

Not that he had anything to offer her. He wasn't the same boy she'd known. That boy was gone.

And in his place …

He didn't want to think about it. He looked up at the mountains in the distance, wondering how easy it would be to disappear. Head home before anyone noticed.

Brandon came out to join him. "Hey man, I wondered where you got to." He leaned against the fence. "What are you doing?"

Josh thought quickly. "Safer out here, away from Kyla's prying eyes."

Brandon laughed. "Kyla's meeting that old family friend of yours. What's the deal with her?"

Josh shrugged. He had to play it cool. "Her family studied here years ago."

Brandon wasn't buying it. "So what's with the 'Aunty, Uncle' thing?"

"Our families were close."

"How close?"

Josh frowned. Brandon would push until he had answers. "They joined us for Fourth of July picnics, Thanksgiving, that kind of thing."

Brandon's look was thoughtful. Josh tried to keep his expression neutral.

"She's a bit full of herself isn't she?"

Josh blinked, offended on Hallie's behalf. Brandon didn't even know her. He calmed himself.

"What makes you think that?"

"I don't know. Her expression. The way she walks. All the big words she uses. That quiet know-it-all voice. She reminds me of that awful woman Mom's cousin married."

"Who?" Brandon didn't talk about his mom's family. The only cousin he talked to was Becky, and she was decent. Always friendly with a bright smile when she saw them.

"Susannah Gilbertson." Brandon said the name as though it left a bad taste in his mouth.

Ah. Becky's mother. From what he knew of the woman she was awful. She thought the world owed her and she was superior to every other living creature. No. There was no comparison between Hallie and Susannah Gilbertson. Josh shook his head. "Hallie's just mature for her age. She's a genius."

Brandon grinned. "Right."

"She is. She finished school early. She's got a degree and she's been working as a librarian in Missouri for years."

Brandon's expression changed. His eyes lighted with interest and Josh wondered why it bothered him. It was better that Brandon was impressed by Hallie than criticizing her, wasn't it?

Brandon slapped him on the back. "Well, this might make life around the lakes a bit more interesting. I heard your mom ask her for lunch. Does that mean you won't be joining us at Joe's?"

Did it? He and Brandon ate at Joe's Diner with Jackson Reilly and his sister most Sundays, along with other friends from church. The Reilly's ranch just out of town demanded a lot of time and it was usually the only chance they had to catch up. But what if Hallie was just passing through?

Brandon read him too well. "Call me after lunch, okay?"

Josh swallowed hard. He didn't know that he wanted to share everything Hallie said or did with Brandon. He drew in a deep breath. He had about ten minutes to get his mind and heart settled before he headed home for lunch.

———

HALLIE WAS INTRIGUED. Something about Brandon sparked her interest. And that scared her. Malcolm had sparked her interest too. She would never allow herself to be so gullible again.

"Where are you staying while you're here?" Aunty Lil asked as she drove Hallie through town.

She'd been invited to lunch and was relieved not to have to walk back to the trailer park in the summer heat.

"I'm in a cabin at the trailer park."

Jodie looked appalled. "You can't stay there. You have to come and stay with us. Doesn't she, Mom?"

"Of course," Aunty Lil said, then smiled. "That is, if she likes our new home."

Aunty Lil pulled into a driveway and Hallie realized why the trailer park had horrified them. She tried not to let her jaw drop, aware that Aunty Lil was watching her.

White rendered bricks encased the front steps and led onto a front porch that looked homey and welcoming. Hallie looked up to see dormer windows facing out from the second story. It had old-world charm.

"It's beautiful." She smiled. "Definitely nicer than where you lived at the college." The brick accommodation buildings had been bland. The main building had been impressive though. Sturdy, strong and timeless. Like this house.

"We couldn't resist." Aunty Lil led Hallie up the path. "Took one look and had to buy it."

A rose garden lined the side fence and vines ran along the walls. It certainly had character. She was sure she'd read a historical romance set in a house like this. Something by Carolyn Miller, maybe.

"What's Esther up to these days?" she asked as Aunty Lil pushed open the front door.

Jodie kicked her shoes off in the entryway. "She's teaching in Spokane. We don't see much of her now she's got a boyfriend." She rolled her eyes. "Probably because Mom keeps pressuring her to get married and provide her with grandchildren."

Aunty Lil laughed. "I do not, Jodie-Lee Ladan."

"What about Josh?" Hallie imagined he was still studying or even pastoring a church somewhere by now.

"He's still at home."

Hallie couldn't mask her surprise. She followed Jodie into the spacious, open-plan living room and her eyes were drawn to the kitchen where a man around her age stood leaning against the bench.

His blue eyes met hers and recognition dawned.

Josh.

"It's Holly!" he said, using the nickname he'd given her as a child. His smile was slow and carefree. "Well, who would believe it?"

Hallie found she couldn't speak. His voice was so deep. He had a slight Australian accent he hadn't had as a child. This was not the Josh she remembered. She'd expected him to have grown up, of course, but she hadn't been prepared for this … this man. His jaw had squared. His shoulders had filled out. His fair hair had darkened, but his eyes were still the same. Still kind. Still knowing, still intelligent. He folded his arms across his chest, and she forced herself to look away. The grown-up Josh had biceps. Probably from playing baseball. Maybe he'd gotten that scholarship into seminary he'd dreamed of as a kid.

"Josh." She managed to acknowledge him.

She liked the way he still used her nickname. He'd claimed nicknames were an honor in Australia, where his mother was from. He'd never called her Hallie for as long as she could remember. She'd liked the name Holly—his play on Hallie Holl-away—and she'd liked him. Now, as she gazed at the grown-up Josh with the cheerful blue eyes and lazy smile, she still liked him.

"Your parents sent us a newsletter the other day," he said, his steady gaze on her, eyes twinkling. "Thought you were a librarian somewhere in Missouri."

She nodded. "I was." She needed to change the subject. "What are you doing these days?"

He chuckled merrily. "Just leaning."

"Exactly," Aunty Lil pulled plates out of the cupboard. "I couldn't have put it better myself. Now, will you stop leaning for a minute and go put these on the table?"

Josh took the plates and haphazardly plopped them on the table one by one. Hallie drew her eyes away from his defined muscles.

"Do you work?" she asked. Maybe he'd answer if she was more specific.

Again, he chuckled. "I'm forced to around here." Then his eyes met hers. "Actually, I've been doing financial and market research and purchase management and a bit of customer care."

"He's a shelf stacker at the supermarket," Jodie called from the living room. She came into the dining room carrying an extra chair. "Don't let him fool you with his fancy talk."

Hallie let out a laugh wondering why someone so intelligent would limit himself to working in a supermarket.

"Jodes finds my real title a bit of a mouthful." Josh rolled his eyes toward Jodie. "She doesn't understand the sacrifice I've made, leaving the more sought-after positions for others. I mean, my job is a tough job, but somebody's got to do it."

Hallie smiled at his droll expression.

He dumped some cutlery onto the middle of the table and shot her a grin. "That'll do. People can get their own."

It confused her. Josh had been a child full of energy and dreams. But now every word, every movement, every action, was carefree and lazy. As though he didn't do anything he didn't have to. In some ways, she envied him. So many people strived to achieve, struggling all their lives to reach the top. Josh appeared content to sit at the bottom, smiling and enjoying every moment.

She could learn something from him.

"Have a seat." He waved his arm toward the chair across from him.

She pulled out the chair and sat. Could she learn to be like him? She was tired of striving, tired of carrying responsibility, tired of meeting peoples' expectations. Josh was lucky. He clearly didn't feel that pressure.

But Lord, is that how you would have me live?

"So Hallie, what are your plans?" Uncle Theo studied her as they ate, his look warm and caring. Hallie had always loved

Uncle Theo. He hadn't changed apart from a few extra gray hairs and a longer beard. He still had that affectionate, fatherly nature. The one she wished her own father had.

"No real plans." Who knew how long until Malcolm was located? The Springfield sheriff hadn't seemed to think he'd risk coming all this way, crossing state borders. "I'm taking time off, seeing where God might lead me. In the meantime, I'm happy to do some volunteer work if you know of any. I'm not good at sitting around doing nothing."

"Unlike some people," Jodie said with a nod toward Josh.

Josh leaned back in his chair and crossed his arms. There were those biceps again. "I'm half Aussie," he said. "I'm allowed to be laid-back. It's in my genes."

Aunty Lil rolled her eyes. "I'm fully Australian, Joshua David Ladan, and you don't see me sitting around doing nothing. Stop giving Aussies a bad name." She looked at Hallie. "What kind of volunteer work were you thinking of?"

Hallie shrugged. "I'm a qualified librarian, but I'd be happy doing anything." Well, mostly. "I really enjoy working with children and I love storytelling, so maybe something along those lines. I've also taught Sunday school. I love seeing children begin to understand God, and I love the way they are so open and innocent. We can learn so much from them."

"Yeah," Josh said around a mouthful. "They don't have to work. They just run around and play and live in the moment." He looked at Aunty Lil pointedly, but she ignored him. She was giving Uncle Theo a meaningful look, and an unspoken message passed between them.

Hallie waited.

Aunty Lil put down her fork. "I think we have just the thing for you. If you're interested, that is."

Uncle Theo smiled, put down the bun he'd been buttering and faced Hallie. "Our church needs a Sunday school teacher, and some of our homeschooling parents could use some support teaching their children."

Hallie blinked. "I … I'm a librarian, not a teacher."

"Yet you were homeschooled. And you enjoy children."

"But I'm not qualified to teach."

"Neither are their mothers. Would you be willing to give it a go?"

Hallie looked around the table. She'd been praying for direction. For God to turn her experience with Malcolm around for good. It seemed God had handed her His answer. "Of course."

Uncle Theo beamed, his eyes crinkling. "Don't you love the way God works?"

"Hey, wait." Josh leaned his elbows on the table. "Who says Holly wants to spend her vacation teaching kids?" He looked steadily across at her. "I mean, you've got potential, Holly. You're a genius, remember?"

Hallie's face heated. It wasn't a title she liked. She'd never liked it. It made her feel too different. Too alone. And it wasn't as though Josh was using his potential. She lowered her eyes, and her voice came out quiet. "What's potential if you don't use it for God's eternal purposes?"

Josh sat back and studied her. "Fair point," he finally said, but his eyes were probing as though he was trying to work something out. She looked away. A lot had happened since they were kids.

"We have to get you out of the trailer park and into Esther's room upstairs," Jodie said as she collected Hallie's plate.

"Wait. What?" That was Josh again. "Why's she coming here?"

Hallie bit her lip. She didn't want to intrude. "Won't Esther need her room when she comes home during vacation?"

Jodie laughed. "She'll be fine, won't she Mom?"

Aunty Lil nodded. "Of course. She'd love you to have her room."

Jodie looked over at Hallie, blonde ponytail bouncing. "If you're worried about Esther, you can sleep in my room when … if she comes home." Jodie grinned. "Just like old times. We can even play Barbies."

Hallie laughed, remembering the innocence of childhood and wishing she could go back. As an only child, playing Barbies with little Jodie had been a joy.

"She can't stay here." Josh's deep voice had them all turning to look at him.

"Why?" Uncle Theo asked.

Josh looked uncomfortable, his eyes darting between them. "It's not right. Not while I'm living here."

"So move out," Jodie said.

Aunty Lil shot her a disapproving look, then her tone turned placating. "She's family, Josh."

"She's not."

Hallie tried not to let his rejection sting, but it did. Josh didn't want her as part of the family. And there was no way she was going to be an inconvenience to those she loved. Not again.

"Maybe not in the eyes of the law, but in our hearts she is," Aunty Lil said quietly, firmly.

Jodie threw a bun across the table at Josh. "You're just worried all your girlfriends will think you've taken up with her and stop coming around."

Josh stood without a word, but his expression was dark. He collected his plate and took it to the sink. Gone was the laid-back Aussie persona.

"I really am fine in the cabin," Hallie said softly.

"No." Aunty Lil's expression was determined. "We want you here, Hallie. You are family." She shot an annoyed look Josh's way, but he'd already left the kitchen.

Hallie bit her lip. Perhaps the Ladan family wasn't as perfect as she'd remembered.

CHAPTER FIVE

Josh felt bad. It wasn't that he didn't like Hallie. It was only she was so … perfect. How was he supposed to feel comfortable and relaxed in his own home with her living there? She was sure to find out he couldn't read. She'd see Mom or Dad helping him or notice he always used text-to-speech on his phone. And what about when a migraine came on? He hated the way they incapacitated him. It was demeaning. He was a grown man, but sometimes he felt like a little boy again.

And Hallie exacerbated that feeling. The way she held her cutlery so delicately. Her neat, precise movements. Her advanced vocabulary and careful way of talking. Her perfect inflection. And the way she'd looked at him when she realized he hadn't followed his dreams to play baseball professionally or become a pastor like his dad. She hadn't looked down her nose at him exactly. She'd just given him that careful look. Intelligent. Knowing. It made him squirm.

He rubbed a hand down his bristled cheeks. He should have shaved before church. No. He didn't need to change because some little girl from his childhood was disappointed in him.

Or was she? Maybe he wasn't being fair. She hadn't said

anything to suggest she was disappointed. Surprised might be a better way to describe what he'd seen behind her cool, calm expression.

She was upstairs now, setting up her few belongings in Esther's room. She hadn't brought much. It was as though she'd left in a hurry, without planning or preparing.

He drew in a breath. He needed to make sure she knew it wasn't her he disapproved of. It was the discomfort of having someone other than family living here. Brandon said visitors were like dead fish—after three days, they started to stink. Not that Hallie would ever stink with whatever that gentle scent she wore happened to be. It wafted along behind her, matching her flowing, graceful walk.

He took the stairs two at a time and leaned on the door frame of Esther's—now Hallie's—room.

"How's it going in here?"

Hallie and Jodie looked up at the same time.

Hallie gave a small smile. "Nearly done." She cleared her throat. "Josh, I promise to keep out of your way. I won't be any trouble."

Josh waved his hand, guilt tightening around his heart. The uncertainty in her expression banished the impression that she was judging him.

"It's no problem. Really. I'm just a selfish man used to his own space. I thought I'd ask if you and Jodie want to come for a walk down along Wainscott Lake with me when you're done. For old times' sake?"

Hallie's blue eyes lit like the summer sky outside. "I'd love to."

Well. That was easy. All forgiven and forgotten.

"Give us ten?" Jodie shooed him away.

His steps were lighter as he came back down the stairs. His phone rang. Brandon. He picked up.

"Hey Brando."

"Josh. What are you up to? How'd it go with your genius friend?"

"Good." He ignored Brandon's snide tone. "We're heading to the lakefront. She loved it as a kid. Want to come?"

What had he done? Things with Hallie were complex in ways he didn't understand and didn't want to explore too closely. Would Brandon pick up on it? What would he think of Hallie? Would he tread on what was precious to her? Brandon was a loyal friend to those he liked, but if he didn't like someone, he didn't hide it.

Brandon laughed. "Sure, I'll come."

Josh's heart sank. "Great. See you there."

JOSH DROVE while Jodie talked to Hallie non-stop, pointing out changes in the town, recounting tales, sharing gossip. Hallie was quiet, but when he glanced in the rearview mirror he saw that she was smiling.

He pulled into the lakeside parking lot. And saw Hallie freeze. She was staring at a silver Honda Accord as it drove past. She looked pale. Flustered.

"That car ..." Her voice was small as she peered out the window. "Did it have Indiana plates?"

Josh squinted, trying to see. "Looks like Washington to me, but we get a lot of tourists here."

"Oh."

"Holly?" He studied her. Something was wrong. She opened the car door.

"Let's walk down by the water. I can't wait." Her voice came out bright. Forced. "You can't know how much I've missed the lakes. Missouri has Lake of the Ozarks, but it's an hour and a half drive from Springfield. I felt like a whole part of me was missing, being so far from the water after living here and then on the island. And now, here I am, back where I've always dreamed of being. Oh. Look at that water."

She was babbling. Not like Hallie at all. He looked at Jodie, eyebrows raised. She shrugged. She had noticed too.

A shiny pickup roared into the parking lot. Brandon.

Jodie shook her head. "He's going to kill somebody one day."

Josh looked at Hallie. "I invited Brandon to come. Hope you don't mind."

"Not at all."

Jodie grinned at her. "Josh and Brandon are like twins. They do everything together. They think the same, talk the same, pick on me the same."

Why'd she have to say that? He was sure Hallie thought little enough of him already.

Brandon jumped out of his maroon Toyota Tacoma with the smart black trim and sauntered over to them.

"Girls. Thought you might like some better company. Classy company."

Josh punched him in the shoulder.

Wisps of red hair flew across Hallie's face as she gave Brandon an appraising look.

"Come on. Let's go." Jodie took Hallie's arm and moved toward the lake's edge.

Brandon looked at Josh. "What's happened?"

Josh sighed. "She's moving in."

"For real?"

"Taking Esther's room."

"But why?"

"She's living in the trailer park and Mom thought ..." He stopped at Brandon's disgusted look.

"The trailer park? What's she doing here anyway? Why isn't she still in her little library in Missouri or wherever she came from?"

"I don't know."

Brandon's gaze went back to Jodie and Hallie. Jodie had taken off her shoes and was walking on the soft grass by the water's edge. Hallie carefully placed each step, appearing to be watching for … dirt? Goose droppings? He wasn't sure.

"So a bit of a mystery?" Brandon asked.

"Maybe."

Brandon fist-pumped the air. "And here I was, getting bored with life here in little ol' Trinity Lakes. I love me a good mystery from Missouri."

Josh looked at Brandon.

Brandon punched his arm. "Come on, man. Don't go all serious on me."

Josh laughed but his gaze returned to the tall red-head walking along the lake's edge beside his sister.

———

HALLIE SMILED as Jodie chattered away, her voice carrying in the summer breeze. The sun reflecting off the water had bite, but she enjoyed it. Trinity Lakes had always felt bright, even in the winter.

"It's good to have a sister here again," Jodie said. "I've missed Esther so much. And Josh and Brandon, well, they're just … Josh and Brandon. They might grow up someday, but I doubt it."

Hallie glanced back at the men trailing behind them. Brandon had Josh in a headlock, dragging him toward the lake. They did seem immature for their age. But at least they were having fun. It was a long time since she'd had fun.

"You don't have many friends you can talk to?"

Jodie sighed. "Not really. I've got plenty of 'friends', but most of them just see me as a way to get close to Josh."

"I'm sure that's not true."

Jodie laughed. "That's sweet of you to say, but you don't look at guys the way other girls do."

She didn't?

Jodie grimaced. "They think I'm stupid. Like I don't know they're more interested in my brother than me. But when they turn up at the door saying they're coming to visit me, then get all pally with Josh and end up talking to him and Brandon the whole time, what am I supposed to think? I try not to, but I resent it."

Hallie nodded. She would resent it too. "I can see how having an irresistible brother and an equally handsome friend could indeed be a disadvantage."

Had she just said that out loud? Jodie's jaw dropped. Apparently she had.

But then Jodie threw her arms around her in a tight hug. "I'm so glad you're back, Hallie. You're a true friend. You're not here to get Josh or Brandon. You're not trying to be someone you're not. You're just Hallie."

Hallie chuckled awkwardly. "You know, Jodie, I don't know that half those girls really want Josh or Brandon either."

Jodie's look was doubtful.

"Think about it. They're flattered by the attention of a handsome man. But who would be happy married to a supermarket shelf stacker with no ambition?"

Jodie stared at her, then looked thoughtful. "I guess I don't need to worry about you falling for Josh, do I?"

"No. No, you don't." Hallie was done with falling for anyone. She wasn't going to be tricked into giving her heart again.

She stopped short. "Who's that?"

Walking along the lakefront was a man with a long scraggly beard and ragged clothes. He dragged a small trailer behind him, which carried a cage containing two waterbirds. Some kind of geese? They squawked and flapped excitedly as the man came closer to the water.

Jodie followed her gaze. "Oh, that's the Junk Man."

"The Junk Man?"

She nodded. "Yeah. The county pays him to pick up trash. And he takes half of it home with him. He's a bit strange."

"So what's he doing with the geese?"

"Releasing them, I think. He finds injured waterbirds and looks after them until they're well enough to return to the wild."

Hallie smiled. "He looks a bit wild himself. What's his real name?"

"I don't know. Everyone calls him the Junk Man."

The man stopped in front of the lake. He bent down and opened the cage, and the two gray birds raced for the water, flapping and cackling. One lifted off, followed by the other. Hallie watched in awe as they soared into the air then came back down onto the lake. The Junk Man stood quietly watching. She couldn't see his expression behind his beard, but she sensed a gentleness in him despite his wild appearance.

"His yard is a complete mess," Jodie said. "He makes shelters out of recycled trash so he can care for all his birds."

Hallie smiled. "So he's actually quite softhearted and clever with his hands?"

Jodie screwed up her nose. "I guess so, but I could think of better things he could do with his soft heart and clever hands."

Hallie wasn't so sure. She admired the way he clearly cared for the birds. A man who loved God's creatures must surely be a gentle, trustworthy soul. Yet, she doubted her ability to judge character. She'd certainly got Malcolm wrong. And it seemed Josh Ladan wasn't who she'd thought he was, either.

Please help me see people the way You see them, Lord. Help me to be discerning.

———

JOSH TRIED NOT to care what Hallie thought, but her harsh judgement hurt. For all her intelligence, she clearly didn't realize how far a voice carried on the breeze off the lake—a pleasant, musical voice that spoke unpleasant truths.

Well, it didn't matter what she thought. He didn't have ambition. That was the truth of it. He wasn't going to be like all the people mindlessly running around to earn more, buy more, have more, never content with what they already had. Contentment was a godly characteristic. The Apostle Paul had it, and Josh had it. Besides, it hurt less not to dream than to have a dream shattered.

Brandon nodded toward the Junk Man. "They should ban him from coming down here. He's supposed to be keeping the lakefront clean, but he's visual pollution. I bet he's got a week's food matted in that beard."

Josh glanced over at the man. He'd always been uncomfortable around the Junk Man, never knowing where to look when the Junk Man glanced his way. His eyes were a piercing green, almost as though they looked through you. And the stories Brandon told him set him on edge.

Apparently the Junk Man's father disappeared under suspicious circumstances while out on the lake with the Junk Man. Josh doubted it was true, but Brandon insisted his mother had inside knowledge.

"He should stay in Frog Swamp. His side of town," Brandon muttered.

Josh rolled his eyes. Brandon and his names for the different parts of town. He'd become less harsh since spending time with Josh's family, but he and his mother could gossip with the best of them. A strange trait for a young man, but Brandon made it seem classy. He said what he thought. And he had been a friend when Josh had needed one most. Brandon hadn't known Josh before his brain injury. Hadn't known the academic Josh who loved baseball. He'd arrived in town to begin his auto apprenticeship a few weeks after Josh arrived home from Australia. Brandon had accepted him as he was while still encouraging him to try new things. It was Brandon who'd gone to the gym with him and encouraged him to continue his physical therapy. Brandon's friendship was a gift from God.

"Come on. Let's go and see Becky," Brandon said. "See if my dear cousin feels like giving away free coffee."

Josh grinned as they made their way to the coffee cart by the side of the lake. If anyone could charm a free coffee out of someone, Brandon could.

Becky Gilbertson smiled at them as they approached the cart with the red candy-striped awning. "No, Brandon, I'm not giving you anything for free."

Brandon leaned against the side of the cart and huffed. "What makes you think I want anything?"

Becky grinned. "Maybe the fact that you ask every time you see me?"

"Yeah. Well." He straightened. "You give the Junk Man free coffee."

Becky stilled. "You know about that?"

Brandon pointed to the nearby tables and chairs under large umbrellas that matched her awning. "He's here when you're setting up in the morning."

"Yeah, well, he deserves the coffee."

Brandon rolled his eyes. "You'd see the good in a lame duck."

Becky nodded. "Exactly. Just like he does. And this lake would be full of trash without him. He does a great service to our town." She looked over at Jodie and Hallie as they came to join them. "Hello, ladies. Would you like a complimentary coffee?"

Jodie beamed. "I'd love one. Thank you."

Brandon made a choking noise. "What? You're unbelievable, Becky."

Becky grinned at him. "I always welcome friendly customers who don't take me for granted." She looked at Hallie. "I don't remember seeing you around. Are you visiting?"

Hallie smiled. "Yes, although I lived here for a few years when I was a child."

Becky's eyes lit with interest. "You must be around my age. What's your name?"

"Hallie Hollaway."

Becky frowned as though trying to place her. "Were you homeschooled?"

"Yes, but I met you a couple of times at the combined churches Christmas carols and Fourth of July fireworks."

Becky's eyes grew wide. "Wow. Do you have a photographic memory or something?"

"She's a genius," Brandon said, shooting a look at Josh.

Josh didn't know where to look. Hallie obviously hadn't liked him calling her that at lunchtime. He'd seen the way she withdrew.

Becky laughed, obviously not believing him. "Welcome home, Hallie. How do you like your coffee?"

CHAPTER SIX

Hallie sat in Esther's bedroom, now her bedroom, and gazed out the window. Trinity Lakes had to be the most beautiful place in the world. She couldn't see the lake, but the summer air felt fresh and alive. She'd only been here a few days, yet she felt right at home.

Her phone rang. With a smile, she picked it up.

"Amanda. How are you going?"

"Hallie." Amanda's tone was serious. "Has Detective Cole called you yet?"

Hope filled Hallie. "No. Have they arrested Malcolm?"

"No. But someone broke into the library. They went through the staff records."

Hallie's heart dropped. "Why? Do you think …?"

"The police have taken prints, and we're waiting to hear back."

"My file didn't say I was coming here, did it?"

"No, of course not. But some people from church know where you've gone. I think we should tell the church members to be wary of anyone asking about you."

Hallie tensed as Simone came to mind. "No. No, I don't want everyone knowing I was so—"

"Don't say stupid. You were trusting."

She'd been going to say gullible, but okay.

Amanda's voice came again. "Have you thought of dyeing your hair?"

"Pardon?"

"It's rather distinctive, Hallie. It might be worth doing." Amanda sounded serious.

Hallie bit her lip and made squiggle patterns on the beautiful quilt Aunty Lil had placed over her bed. "I'll think about it."

"Thank you." Amanda sounded relieved. "I'm praying for you, Hallie. Missing you."

An unexpected lump came to her throat. She missed Amanda too. And the library. And the loss of the sense of security. For the second time in her life.

"God bless, Amanda. Thanks for looking out for me."

"Always. I'm praying for you. Stay safe, Hallie."

Hallie ended the call and sat looking at her new phone, glad she'd left her old one with the police. *I don't want to live in fear, looking over my shoulder. Lord, please protect me and show me what to do.*

"No, Hallie. I'm not doing it." Jodie crossed her arms. "Don't give me that look. There is no way I'm changing your hair color. It's … it's you."

Hallie winced. "What if I want a new me?"

Jodie shook her head and sat on the edge of her bed. "Hallie, you're beautiful just the way you are."

Why did that sound so patronizing? Maybe because she didn't believe it? Maybe because she could still hear the taunts of other children when she'd first arrived in Trinity Lakes. She'd wanted to hide, but her appearance had made her stand out. She could still remember Josh defending her, telling the children to leave her alone. He'd been a whole year older and popular. He could have chosen to spend time with anyone, but he'd befriended her. Red hair and all.

But this wasn't about appearance. It was about safety.

"I can go down to the hair salon if you'd prefer not to do it."

Jodie studied her a moment then sighed. "I'll do it, but only if you're sure."

"I'm sure."

Jodie fingered Hallie's hair. "The blonde I use won't work. The red will show through. We'll need to go darker. I have some of the dark brown I use on Mom's hair. We can do a strand test if you like."

Hallie smiled. She liked the color of Aunty Lil's hair. She drew in a deep breath. "Let's do this."

She refused to second-guess her decision as Jodie took her into the bathroom, put on gloves, and began the process. Hallie hadn't realized coloring hair was such a serious business.

Hallie closed her eyes. Today, her new life began. A new home. A new family. A new job. No more searching for love from a man. It was too much to hope for a marriage like Uncle Theo and Aunty Lil's. They'd met and married at Trinity Lakes Bible College many years ago, and their love for God and each other was obvious. Josh might be their son, but he was as different from Uncle Theo as he could be, almost as if he tried to be that way. He'd changed since he was a boy.

And so had she.

Two hours later, Hallie stared at herself in the mirror. Her hair looked … strange. She looked … like lots of other people. Wasn't that what she'd always wanted? To fit in? To blend in with the crowd? She pulled down a strand of the now-mahogany colored hair.

"I like it."

Jodie nodded. "I do, too. It makes your eyes stand out more."

Hallie glanced in the mirror at her eyes. It did. But it also made her freckles look misplaced. She turned back to Jodie.

"Can you teach me to put on makeup?" Her mother had never taught her, having never worn it herself.

"You don't need it, Hallie."

"I want it."

Jodie grinned. "Okay. Come to my room and we'll do a complete makeover."

"Thank you."

Jodie giggled throughout the makeover as she tried different shades against Hallie's skin tone. Hallie enjoyed herself—she may even have giggled a time or two. Jodie taught her how to put on her own makeup and Hallie relished the feeling of sisterly connection. Who would have thought that someday Jodie would take on the role of big sister and help her?

When they'd finished, Hallie gave Jodie an impulsive hug. "Thank you."

Jodie beamed. "I'm so glad you're here, Hallie. I miss having a big sister. Esther hardly comes home anymore and Josh ... well, Josh is Josh."

Hallie knew exactly what she meant.

———

"WHAT HAVE YOU DONE?" Josh stared at Hallie. She now looked like every other girl he knew. He spun to face Jodie. "You talked her into this, didn't you?"

Hallie spoke. "No, Josh, this was all my idea." She gave him a calm, placating smile. It was infuriating.

Jodie lifted her chin. "She's an adult. She can make her own choices. She doesn't tell you to put on some decent clothes, does she? Or complain because Brandon comes here after work with his jeans covered in grease?"

Josh narrowed his eyes. "I think you just did."

Hallie's look turned troubled as she stepped between them and faced him. "I never even thought to say anything about what you wear because appearance doesn't matter," she said. "What matters is where the heart lies."

Had she just preached at him? "Yeah. Well. I think Jodie's heart lied when it said you'd look better as a plastic brunette."

Hallie flinched and he felt awful. He shouldn't have said that. He was acting like Brandon, speaking his mind without considering who it might hurt. Hallie had already been hurt enough.

He'd never forget the day she'd admitted to him that other kids teased her about her hair, made her feel ugly. He'd stood up for her, tried to convince her she was exactly the way God made her. As a nine-year-old boy, he hadn't been able to bring himself to say she was beautiful, even though it was the truth. Why did Hallie coloring her hair feel like a personal rejection?

Hallie's shoulders straightened and she looked positively regal. Her blue eyes pierced his. "I'll have you know that I don't need your good opinion. I am not a helpless child, and you are not my big brother. We're not family, remember?"

He winced. The only reason he'd insisted she wasn't family was … No. Best not go there.

"You'd do well to remember that." She pivoted on her heel and marched away while Jodie stood looking at him, eyes accusing.

He shook his head, clicked his tongue and stalked out the door Hallie hadn't taken. She was a far cry from the sweet little girl he'd been friends with all those years ago.

She'd been so sweet despite the neglect and rejection she suffered. He'd never forget the day he'd realized just how awful her home life was. He'd never liked Mr. Hollaway. Never been able to call him Uncle the way Hallie called Dad Uncle. Dad tried to tell him it was just Mr. Holloway's way. That he wasn't good with children. He'd wondered why the Hollaways had Hallie then. Until it all became clear.

Nine-year-old Hallie had been given a new kitten and she was delighted with it. Her blue eyes lit up and her smile was filled with joy.

But Mr. Hollaway grumbled about it constantly. "Don't come crying to me when it runs out on the road and gets itself killed," he'd said one day. Mom looked horrified.

But that was exactly what happened. Josh had gone to ask Hallie's parents if she could come for dinner when he'd spotted her. She stood by the side of the road, sobbing her heart out as her father bent down behind his car, picked up a small, furry form and threw it into the trash can. Then she charged away, her little-girl cries breaking his heart.

Mr. Hollaway glanced after her, then looked at Josh, his mouth grim. "I told her it would happen. It's a good lesson for her." Then he'd gotten back in his car and driven away.

And Josh found himself fighting hatred for the father who showed no compassion for his daughter.

It had taken a while to find Hallie. Her sobs led him to the bush in her backyard. She was curled up beneath it, tears streaking through the dust on her face, joining her freckles together in one large, brown mass.

"He hates me," she'd said, her voice breaking. "That's why he did it."

An awful feeling settled deep in his gut, but he wrapped his arms around her. "No, Holly, that's not true."

"It is."

"I'm sure it was an accident."

"No, he didn't like Muffin, and he doesn't like me. I heard him tell Mr. Carrigan that he and Mom didn't want children. He said I was an unpleasant surprise."

"Oh, sweetheart." The endearment came naturally. It was

what his own mother called him when she comforted him. It was what Dad called Mom.

"Now Muffin is gone, I have no one. No one loves me."

"We love you," he'd said. "Mom, Dad, Esther, me, Jodie. We all love you."

She'd looked up at him with such hope. Such desperation to be loved. She'd clung to him. She'd needed him. And the adoration in her big blue eyes had touched his little boy heart in a way he'd never forget.

But she didn't need him anymore. She was an adult. A strong, independent woman who'd made it clear what she now thought of him. Her dark hair and clear skin devoid of freckles was yet another sign she'd changed—that things had changed between them.

He wished he didn't care so much.

CHAPTER SEVEN

Hallie watched the Browns' foster son race around the room. He was hyper, but at least when he was running, he wasn't hitting or biting himself. Her first day helping home-school the children next door was not what she'd expected.

"Miss Holliwen?" The little boy stopped long enough to look up at her. "You catch me?"

Poor kid. His foster mother had insisted they call her "Miss Hollaway." It was a mouthful for such a small child.

He tugged on her hand. She laughed. "Not right now, Jimmy. I'm supposed to be helping Eden and Abella with their writing."

The little boy's eyes filled. Her heart softened. "Well, just for a minute, okay?"

She hadn't realized the job would require so much play. She chased Jimmy around the room. He ducked under a desk, then backed himself into a corner. With a laugh, she came after him. Then stopped. He'd gone completely still, terror filling his eyes.

Slowly, she backed away, speaking softly. "It's okay, Jimmy. We're just playing. It's just a game."

Jimmy stared up at her, unblinking.

"He gets scared easy," Eden said.

"Easily," Hallie corrected, then bit her lip. It was too easy to be in academic teaching mode. These children needed more than knowledge. They needed love. They needed Jesus.

She looked at Eden and Abella. "Girls, why don't you put down your pens? I think it's time for a story."

Eden and Abella had no trouble snuggling up to Hallie's side. She put her arms around each of them while Jimmy stayed in the corner.

"It's about lions," Hallie said quietly. "And how God looks after us."

Eden played with a strand of Hallie's now dark hair. "Is it from the Bible?"

"It is."

All three children sat perfectly still as Hallie told them the story.

"So God can even stop hungry lions," she said to finish the story. "We don't need to be afraid. Even if we feel like we're surrounded by lions. We can always talk to God. He's always here, and he loves us. He's the one who saves us."

Abella pulled her knees up under her chin. "God didn't stop the police taking my parents away, Miss Hollaway."

Hallie bit her lip. What was she supposed to say to that? Every answer she came up with sounded trite. Instead, she pulled Abella in closer.

"Have you ever been scared, Miss Hollaway?" Eden's eyes searched hers, seeking truth. Seeking connection.

"I have."

"What happened?"

Hallie's mind worked fast. There was no way she would tell them about Malcolm. But could she tell them about what had happened when she was ten?

Lord?

Peace filled her. God had protected her. She was here. Safe.

"When I was a child, my parents were missionaries on an

island. One day, some people there got very angry. They wanted to kill me and my parents. I remember praying in my mind, over and over. I prayed 'Please God, send them away, please God send them away.' I thought maybe they'd disappear or go blind like the army who tried to attack Israel." She grinned. "That's a story for another day. Anyway, God didn't make them go away like I asked Him to. I couldn't understand why. But they didn't kill us and my parents and I were able to come safely home."

Abella stared up at Hallie, her eyes bright. "I want to go overseas one day. I want to go to Australia, where Mrs. Ladan comes from."

"Mrs. Ladan talks funny," Eden said.

"Eden." Abella glared at her sister. "That's rude."

Eden's gaze shot to Hallie who smiled to reassure her. "It's called an accent."

"I like the way she talks," Abella said. "I want to go to Australia and see a kangaroo. Jodie told me they went to Australia to visit their grandparents and saw kangaroos."

Hallie noticed that Jimmy was inching closer. "We had books about Australian animals in the library I worked in," she said. "There are some amazing creatures over there. Like the crazy platypus. God made it with a duck's bill and it lays eggs, but it's actually a mammal."

Now she had their rapt attention. She pulled out her phone to find a picture.

HALLIE WAS EXHAUSTED when the day ended. But she'd had fun. Eden and Abella waved her goodbye, while Jimmy came to her side and tugged on the bottom of her shirt.

"Miss Holliw ... Holli ..."

She knelt down to his level. "You can call me Miss Holly."

He nodded, his big brown eyes serious. "Miss Holly, can God take off my dad's arm?"

Hallie blinked. What was she supposed to say to that?

"Why would you want Him to do that, sweetheart?"

Jimmy's eyes filled. "I want to go home, but I don't want him to hit me anymore."

"Oh, Jimmy." Hallie desperately wanted to pull him into her arms, but she wasn't sure if that was the right protocol. "I think it would be good for you to talk to your foster mom about that. What do you think?"

He nodded, then reached for her hand. He gave it a squeeze then ran back inside. Hallie stared after him, her heart breaking.

How could parents treat their children like that? What gave them the right?

Lord, I have no idea how to deal with this. Give me wisdom.

Her job no longer seemed like play. The weight of her responsibility felt enormous.

Hallie walked down the path and opened the front gate.

How do I help them, Lord?

"Hallie?" Her attention was drawn to the Ladans' driveway. Aunty Lil leaned out her car window. "I'm about to head down to the shops. Do you want to come?"

She desperately wanted to go up to Esther's room and relax, but there were some essentials she needed from the grocery store. She opened the passenger side door.

"Thank you."

Aunty Lil smiled, waiting until Hallie buckled up her seatbelt. "How'd your day go?"

Hallie blinked. Saw the understanding in Aunty Lil's eyes.

"It was hard. Those children ... they're so wounded. They've lost their innocence so young. I don't know how to help them. I feel like all I'm doing is playing with them and telling them stories when they need so much more."

"Do they?" Aunty Lil backed out onto the road. "Or do they need a childhood?"

Hallie stared out the front windshield, the scenery beginning to blur.

"Sweetheart?" Aunty Lil reached over and gently touched Hallie's arm. It was her undoing.

"How can I help them have a childhood when I didn't have one? I don't know how to be a child. I don't know how to give them what they need."

Aunty Lil pulled off the road into a side street. She took off her seatbelt and turned to face Hallie.

"Give them what you missed out on."

"But how do I know what that is?"

Aunty Lil smiled gently. "What do you think it is?"

Hallie looked out the windshield, blinking hard. Innocence. Love. Joy. Fun. Acceptance. Her father's face came to mind, and she remembered the many nights she'd lain awake wondering where her parents were and who they were helping. As her tears flowed through those lonely nights, she had wondered what made those people more important, more lovable than her.

"Hallie, can I be completely open with you?" Aunty Lil's eyes were warm and caring. Accepting.

"Please do."

"People are always more important than ministry. People *are* ministry. All people. I think your parents may have lost sight of that, not because they didn't love you, but because they didn't know how to show it. They didn't know how to meet the needs of a child."

"They didn't even want a child."

Aunty Lil's eyes widened. "Did they say that?"

Hallie's chin quivered. "I heard Dad say it."

Aunty Lil's eyes filled with tears. "Oh, my dear girl, I can't begin to imagine how that must have hurt."

Hallie pulled a tissue out of her bag, then faced Aunty Lil

again. "I'm not a genius like people think, Aunty Lil. Do you know why I finished school so early?"

Aunty Lil's eyes filled with compassion, urging her to go on.

"Because I was an inconvenience to my parents' ministry. I held them back. The sooner I finished school, the sooner they could get on with God's work."

"Oh, Hallie." Aunty Lil reached across the console of the car and pulled Hallie into a tight hug. "You could never be an inconvenience. You were their ministry."

Hallie shook her head. "No, I wasn't. They couldn't love me. Not like they love the islanders. Not like they love those they're leading to Jesus. And you know the worst of it? I felt terrible being jealous of those people they were leading to Jesus. I felt selfish for wanting their time and attention when I was already going to heaven. I have eternal life. That should be enough."

"But it wasn't enough, was it?" Aunty Lil's eyes looked into hers. She laid a gentle hand on her cheek. "Because children have a need to be loved by their parents."

And there was the catch.

Aunty Lil handed her another tissue. "Hallie, it's not that you're not lovable. It's not that you don't deserve attention. It's that your parents didn't know how to love you. And that's not your fault. That's not on you. Don't ever think it is."

But that was the problem. She did. Who could love her when her parents couldn't even love her?

It was as though Aunty Lil read her thoughts. "Do you blame the Browns' foster children for the way their parents treated them?"

"No, but ..."

"No buts, Hallie. They've been wounded. You were wounded. And it wasn't your fault. The Healer is waiting, longing to bring healing deep in your heart. And the best way to do that is to love those children. Love them 'til it hurts and until every one of your own hurts is washed away in the love of Jesus that you share with them."

"I don't think I can do that."

"Or you don't think God can do that?" Aunty Lil's eyes searched hers. "Do you trust Him, Hallie? Because Jesus loves those children and He's the one who will be doing the healing. You love the children in His name. Can you do that?"

"I don't know. I know God can do it, but …"

"Don't believe He will?"

Hallie looked down at the tissue scrunched in her hand. "No, I guess I don't."

"Well, if you don't believe it, I suspect you won't be praying toward that end. Nor will you be taking steps to be a part of the process. God chooses to use us when we're available. Don't miss out because of lack of faith, Hallie."

Hallie sniffed. She rested her hand on top of Aunty Lil's. "Can we pray?" she whispered.

Aunty Lil smiled. "Of course." And she bowed her head and prayed, while Hallie let herself truly pour out her heart to God, believing He loved her. That He would answer.

CHAPTER EIGHT

"Josh?"

He looked up from his video game as Hallie tapped him on the shoulder. He hadn't heard her enter the basement. He took off his headphones and hit the pause button.

"Yeah?" It had been over a week, and he still couldn't get used to her dark hair. At least she'd stopped using makeup. She looked less intimidating with freckles. Cute even. But he'd never tell her that.

"What time do you finish work tomorrow?"

He turned his chair to fully face her. "Around two. Why?"

"The Browns' foster kids have been asking about Australia, so we've been looking into everything Australian."

"And you want me over there as a prime example of a fine Aussie man?"

She almost smiled. Almost. "No. Tomorrow we'll be writing stories about Australian animals, and I thought you could help."

His heart missed a beat and sank at the same time. "Help them write their stories?"

"Yes. And give them ideas. After all, you've been to Australia a few times to visit your grandparents. There's nothing like firsthand knowledge."

He'd known this would happen. Of all the things she could have asked him to do. He couldn't say yes. She'd find out he couldn't read, and he couldn't bear her knowing. Not when she was so clever, when her whole career as a librarian centered around reading and writing. But if he said no, it would confirm her opinion that he was lazy.

Esther had already tried to teach him to read again when she'd been at college training to be a teacher. Poor Esther. He'd been a huge disappointment. She'd even prayed for healing for him as she tried. And he'd prayed and believed. At first. But as his frustration mounted, his migraines grew more intense. Now, four years after his accident, they had to believe the neurologist's prognosis. Alexia was permanent. That pathway in his brain was gone. Dead. He needed to keep his life as stress-free as possible.

Right now, looking into Hallie's hopeful eyes, stress-free was not the way he'd describe his life.

He looked back at the screen where his video game remained paused, the text-to-speech option highlighted. Would she notice? "Sorry, I have another commitment."

He did now, anyway. He'd deliver the groceries he'd been putting together for the elderly gentleman who'd stopped and talked with him at work while he was stocking shelves yesterday. He'd just lost his wife, poor man.

Hallie was looking at him like she didn't believe him. Well, let her think what she liked. That was on her, not on him.

She hadn't seen him in an Australian hospital with a tube draining excess fluid from his brain, with paralysis of one side of his face due to swelling. She hadn't seen him have to wipe away drool he couldn't control. And she hadn't seen Grandpa by the side of his bed, begging forgiveness.

"I never should have encouraged you to play footy. Not when you

haven't been taught how to handle a tackle. I'm so sorry, Josh. So sorry."

And Josh had tried to tell him it was okay. That he'd wanted to learn Aussie Rules football. That he hadn't seen the big Aussie halfback coming at him. But he couldn't speak. His mouth wouldn't work. He was trapped in his own body, all his dreams for life shattered and replaced with fear. He couldn't live like this. Didn't want to live like this.

Mom, Dad, Esther, and Jodie had needed to go back home. He'd understood that. He'd even insisted Mom leave when she tried to work out a way to stay. Yet he couldn't quash the feeling of abandonment. Grandma and Grandpa stayed with him for the months of rehabilitation. No one knew how hard it was. The paralysis wasn't permanent and the swelling had gone away, but his mind didn't work the way it used to. Most people couldn't tell, but he could feel it. And there was nothing worse than looking at words on a page, unable to process what he was seeing.

Thank God for Brandon. He'd arrived at church the same day Josh finally gathered up the courage to return after arriving back from Australia. The two connected immediately and left no room for church members to ask about the accident or why he'd been in Australia for so long. He'd asked his family not to give details.

He'd felt guilty for blaming being half Aussie for his slower speech and his appearance of laziness. The truth was, although he might appear like a duck swimming calmly on the surface, he was paddling like crazy underneath. Struggling to hide his disability, struggling to act like he'd enjoyed a year-long vacation in Australia, struggling to forget the months of pain and rehabilitation.

Brandon had been there when a migraine hit at church the following Sunday. He'd taken him home and Josh had admitted the extent of his condition. Brandon hadn't looked shocked, hadn't pitied him. He'd accepted it and accepted him.

Hallie hadn't moved. He risked one last glance at her and found the pinched expression of confusion and disappointment he'd expected.

"All right then." She wrapped her arms around her middle. "But if you change your mind, we'd love to have you."

————

HALLIE LEFT Josh to his video game. She tried not to be annoyed. Maybe he wasn't good with kids. Maybe he was scared he wasn't sensitive enough to respond appropriately to such damaged, wounded children. She'd been nervous at first, but she loved her job more every day.

A knock came at the door and Hallie answered.

Brandon stood there with Rachel. She opened the door. "Josh is in the basement."

"Thanks." Brandon headed downstairs with Rachel in tow. The Ladan home seemed to be the unofficial gathering place of many young females in the church, but Jodie was right. They were only here to see Josh.

Not that she blamed them. She understood why. He could be a lot of fun. Despite his faults, he'd never lost the kindness he'd had when he was young. He had an ability to make her feel noticed that no one else had. The problem was, he made everyone feel noticed, including every girl in church. Maybe she should move out, find a place of her own where she could curl up in solitude with a good book.

She pulled out her phone. Surely there'd be somewhere she could rent, somewhere apart from the trailer park cabin?

Rachel came up the stairs, giggling. Brandon and Josh were close behind. Hallie avoided rolling her eyes when Rachel leaned into Josh as though she'd lost her balance and he put his arm out to hold her steady. He would do that for anyone, so why did it bother her so much? After all, she didn't want Josh herself. Couldn't want Josh. They were too different. Josh had no ambition and his heart for God was, well, questionable.

Besides, she'd learned her lesson from Dave. Malcolm. Whoever he was.

"See you tomorrow night, Josh," Rachel said and her expression was positively mushy.

Josh nodded and smiled. "Looking forward to it."

The door closed behind Rachel, and Brandon plopped onto the sofa across from Hallie.

"Did you hear that girl?" Brandon imitated her giggle.

Hallie wanted to be disgusted, but it was such a good impression that she couldn't help a smile peeking through. She glanced at Josh. Would he defend Rachel?

No, he sat down beside Hallie with an easy smile and a twinkle in his eyes, then made an outrageous sound.

"That's how an Australian kookaburra laughs," he said.

Nice deflection. But he should have stood up for Rachel the way he'd stood up for her years ago when other children teased her. Why didn't Josh ever go against Brandon? Did he no longer have any convictions, any courage?

Josh made the kookaburra sound again and nudged her in the side. "Come on, Hallie. You try it."

She refused, but couldn't help laughing when Brandon joined in, making the most disgusting laugh noises she'd ever heard. Then she covered her mouth. The last thing she wanted was for Brandon to mock her laugh too.

If only Josh and Brandon weren't so likable despite their faults. It would make life easier. They weren't good for each other, the way they went from acting like gossipy old ladies to immature little boys.

Brandon finally left to go home.

Josh leaned over to look at Hallie's phone. "What are you doing?"

She pulled away. "Looking for a place to rent." She scrolled down the list of available options. There were many in the new housing estate, but all too pricey for her.

"So you're staying in Trinity Lakes?"

She nodded.

"Why?"

She didn't answer. She wasn't going to tell him about Malcolm. Or the fact that she hadn't fit in Springfield. That she'd had no friends her own age.

Josh took out his phone. "Let me help you."

Was he trying to make up for refusing to help her with the Brown children? She tried to ignore him despite the way he sat so close, his arm brushing against hers. Then he let out a hoot and held out his phone.

"I've found the perfect home for you."

"I'm sure you have." Hallie glanced at his phone before going back to her own.

"I have. Holly, how could you doubt me?"

She allowed herself a small smile. "I thank you for your effort, but I'm not sure I want you picking a home for me."

"Come on, Holly. It's a lovely little cottage and it's only a twenty-minute walk from here so you won't miss me too much. It has two bedrooms, a decent yard, and plenty of room for the Junk Man to throw his trash over the fence if he runs out of room on his side."

Now she was interested. "It's next door to the Junk Man?"

Josh chuckled mischievously. "Yeah, but don't let that put you off. No one has been able to stay there for long, but you're tough, Holly. I know you could do it."

"I could," she said, and was unable to contain her laugh at the look that came to Josh's face. He obviously hadn't thought she would consider it. "I like the Junk Man. I think he's fascinating, and he's obviously got a good heart."

"And a disgustingly messy house and yard and dirty habits."

"And you don't?"

Josh pulled a face. "Ooh, that hurt." Then he grinned. "At least I've got a mother to make me clean up. Come on, Holly. You're not seriously considering it, are you? I was just joking."

Hallie leaned over to look at his phone. "I know you were joking, but I think I should at least check it out. You don't want me hanging around here forever, do you?"

He threw an arm around her shoulder. "I dunno. It would save me having to chase all those girls away. I could tell them you and I are together or something."

She stiffened at his touch. Tried to clear her head. Having Josh the man put his arm around her was different to when Josh the boy had held her and comforted her. So different.

She cleared her throat. "I haven't seen you attempt to chase any girls away. And dating Rachel hasn't stopped other girls coming around, has it?"

Josh leaned in closer, his eyes sparkling. "No, but you're different. They know they can't compete with you. And we could take it to the next level—get unofficially engaged or married or something."

Hallie shook her head. Josh had made an art of flirting. He hardly even realized he was doing it, it came so naturally. She was just another girl he flirted with and that annoyed her. On the other hand, she couldn't help responding and that was embarrassing. He certainly had a way about him, and the safest thing was to treat him like her brother, so that no one, not even he, could believe he had the slightest effect on her.

"You wouldn't want to marry me, Josh. You'd have to give up all your other girlfriends and grow up. I don't think you could live with that."

Was that hurt that flashed over his face? If it was, it disappeared as quickly as it came.

"Oh, I don't know. You could teach me a lot. Make me clean up after myself, chastise me when I'm selfish or childish. Make a man out of me."

Warmth crept up into Hallie's face. Did she really treat him like a child? She didn't mean to. It was just … easier. It helped her keep her distance. To guard her heart.

She stood. "I'm going to go and check out this cottage."

For the first time, Josh looked concerned. "I'm sure there's somewhere better for you."

Hallie smiled. "What if this is where God wants me? Even the Junk Man needs Jesus."

Josh frowned. "This is the US, Hallie. You can't just go preaching at people like you did on the mission field. People don't like being told what to do or being lectured. They know when someone is looking down on them."

Hallie drew in a deep breath. "You think I do that?"

His eyes widened as though he hadn't realized what he'd said. Then his voice softened. "You can come across that way sometimes."

Pain slashed her chest. She would not cry. She would not. "Who are you to talk? You're the one who just said all those terrible things about the Junk Man." She held back her tears. "And what about you and Brandon with all your mocking, snide remarks? At least I'm trying to love people. At least I make an effort to look outside myself to the world out there in need. You and Brandon just watch the world go by as if it's there for your entertainment. You smirk and gossip and treat people like dirt. This is my chance to find a life of my own. To find a place I belong."

Josh reeled back. Blinked. "Well," he said. "I hope you find what you're looking for."

Hallie's nose stung. She screwed it up, closed her eyes. "Josh …"

No response. She opened her eyes. He was gone.

What had she done? She couldn't believe she'd snapped at Josh that way.

She squeezed her eyes shut. *Lord …?*

Josh stirred up feelings in her she couldn't control. Disappointment. Grief. Longing. And yes, desire.

It would be dangerous to grow fond of Josh again. Yet she couldn't seem to help it.

She moved to the kitchen. She needed a drink of water. Needed to calm down and sort out her crazy feelings. She stopped at the door. Josh leaned on the kitchen bench. His broad shoulders were hunched, muscles rippling beneath his black cotton t-shirt. His head was bowed.

She'd done that to him.

"Josh?" Her chin quivered.

He turned his head. His eyes were sad, his usual smile absent. It broke her heart.

He straightened and turned around to face her. "Holly, I know you don't think much of me, but I can't let you talk about Brandon like that. He's a good guy."

Hallie shook her head, but Josh stepped toward her. "He is. I know he can be insensitive, but if you understood his family life, what he's been through … He's always been there for me. He's the best friend I've ever had."

Why did that hurt? Why did she want to own that role? She was being ridiculous again. She bit her lip. "Josh, I'm sorry for what I said about both you and Brandon." Her eyes filled.

"But did you mean it?"

She blinked, trying to see his expression through eyes blurred with tears. She could lie to him. But she wouldn't.

"I like you Josh. I always have. You're great fun. You can be so compassionate. You were there at a time in my childhood when I needed you."

His smile was sad. "But you don't need me now. You're all grown up and you don't need anyone."

"Except God." It came out whisper-soft.

Josh nodded. "Don't we all?"

She held his gaze. Tried to see what was going on behind his troubled eyes. He held out his hand.

"Can we be friends again? Like before?"

"You mean like when we were kids?"

He smiled. "I do childhood much better than I do adulthood. So … yes?"

She smiled back, her heart easing. "Of course." She held out her hand. As his strong, manly hand clasped hers, she knew that no matter how much they wished it, there was no going back to childhood.

CHAPTER NINE

Hallie knew the real estate agent wasn't giving her the full picture as she was shown through the cottage. It was plain but delightful, with polished floorboards and old-fashioned windows. No mention was made of the Junk Man. Every now and then his birds began an excited gaggle of sound, but the agent only blinked as though ignoring it would mean it wasn't happening.

For Hallie's purposes, the cottage was perfect. Close enough to the Ladans' that she could walk, far enough away that she had her independence. And it was affordable. The Brown family insisted on paying her, so she had money coming in, and she still had some savings left. She signed the rental agreement as soon as she was approved.

Some people from church brought second-hand furniture to fill the space. Brandon was conspicuously absent. Jodie said he'd ranted and raved about how the Junk Man would murder her in her sleep, but he hadn't said it to her directly. Hallie wondered why he despised the Junk Man so fiercely.

Josh hung around as furniture was brought in, generally

getting in everyone's way but being so entertaining no one complained.

"I think this little ornament thing looks great right here." He tapped the washing machine which stood in the center of the kitchen, ready to be moved to the laundry room. "It definitely suits your décor. Matches the white of this thing." He pointed to the dryer. "Not sure what it is, but it looks good. Useful, maybe."

Aunty Lil laughed. "She won't need it much. I saw a clothesline out the back. Best way to dry laundry in the warmer months. Natural, and environmentally friendly."

Jodie rolled her eyes. "Anyone would think we're in Australia with all the clotheslines here in Trinity Lakes."

Hallie had seen the line strung across between two poles in the back yard and wondered what they were. Now she knew. She might even try using it.

Josh bent down and took a wastepaper basket from a half-empty box. "And this thing—what is it?" He held it up. "Now, let's see … where's the hat rack?" He put the basket on his head. It hung over his eyes, and he walked straight into a wall.

Hallie was sure he'd done it on purpose, but he managed to look stunned.

"That's my wastepaper basket." She reached to take it from his head, but he ducked out of the way.

"Oh." He threw her a dopey grin. "You use a wastepaper basket, do you? Wouldn't it be easier to just sweep the floor once a week on trash day? Then you can sweep it all right off the back step and straight into the trash can."

"Oh, Josh," his mother said. "I hate to think how you'd live if you were on your own."

"He'd definitely be on his own, that's for sure," Jodie called from where she was putting a set of donated sheets into the linen cupboard. "Nobody could stand to live with him."

Josh removed the basket from his head. "Brandon would."

"Only because he's tidy and would do all the picking up for you."

That Brandon was tidy was news to Hallie.

Jodie tapped on the side window. "Have you met the Junk Man, Hallie?"

"Not yet."

Josh groaned. "I can't believe you'd choose to live next door to him. Brandon says you've got to be crazy."

Hallie screwed up her nose. "And why would I care what Brandon thinks?"

Josh laughed. "Don't pretend you don't. All the girls do."

Hallie placed a toaster donated by the Carrigan family at church on her kitchen counter. "Not me."

Josh's gaze caught hers. "You know what, I believe you."

———

JOSH SIGHED as he looked up from his phone and gazed out his bedroom window. It was too quiet. He missed having Hallie around. Missed her voice. He'd been searching his text-to-speech app to find a voice like hers. He was tired of the stilted male voice that read his texts to him. But no female voice he found was quite like hers.

He groaned. What was wrong with him? There was no way Hallie would ever take an interest in him, especially if she knew he couldn't read. He'd seen her excitement as she'd unpacked a box of books donated by Tabby from the Lakeview Inn.

It was best Hallie was out of the house. At least she was still in town. But for how long? He was worried about her financial situation. Would she eat well now she wasn't living with them? When she was staying in Esther's room, she'd had her food and board covered. And she deserved that, with all the work she was doing free for the church. He could deliver her some groceries. Surely there was something more he could do.

. . .

JOSH KNOCKED on Dad's office door. Dad looked up and grinned. "Come in, son. Let me guess, you're here because God gave you a sermon and you want to preach it on Sunday?"

Josh plopped into the chair in front of Dad's desk. "You're not funny."

"Sorry." He didn't look sorry. His eyes sparkled with humor. Then his smile faded. "Josh, God has something special for you. You know that, don't you? He doesn't take a dream and leave His children floundering. He has a better plan. A plan better than you ever imagined."

"I know." He fiddled with the envelope in his hands. "Dad, there's something I want to talk to you about."

Dad leaned forward, listening in that intent, caring way of his.

Josh drew in a breath. "I know the church can't pay Hallie for doing Sunday school and the Browns don't pay her much ..."

Dad nodded. "And now she's moved out, she's not getting room and board."

"Exactly. I wondered, is it possible for us to ask church people to donate something financially—the way they donated furniture?"

Dad looked thoughtful. "That's not a bad idea. She can't eat furniture. Not that she can eat money, either." His beard shook.

Josh rolled his eyes. He handed the envelope in his hand to Dad. "This is my contribution."

Dad opened the envelope and glanced in. His eyes widened at the generous amount. He knew how little Josh earned.

Josh looked away, uncomfortable. When he finally met Dad's gaze again, the pride in his father's eyes warmed him.

He pointed the envelope at Josh. "Next time that sister of yours accuses you of not caring for anybody but yourself—"

Josh shook his head. "Please don't say anything. I don't want people to assume that …" He saw the grin peeking through Dad's beard. "Well, can you imagine the rumors that would go around if anyone knew?"

Dad laughed, then sobered. "I know. Too many eyes and ears and tongues in this town."

Josh stretched his legs in front of him and focused on his shoes. "Could you maybe mention the idea at your next church meeting? Get them to pass it around by word of mouth and have people give you their donations in an envelope?"

Dad nodded. "Good idea."

"And don't tell them it was my idea or how much I gave."

"Why?"

Josh knew what he was really asking. He rubbed the back of his neck. He'd thought out an acceptable answer. One that satisfied him and should satisfy Dad. "Because she deserves it. Because she's helping the whole church, and the Brown family. And, well, she's never really been looked after. Her parents are so focused on their mission work …"

He glanced at Dad, who nodded in understanding. "I know. It's always troubled me. I was glad they let her spend so much time at our place, but it was only because it got her out of their hair, not because they knew how much she needed us."

Josh sighed. "But now she doesn't want us." Or him, anyway. "I get that I'm hard to live with, but it hurts to think she moved out because of me."

Dad tapped a pen on his desk. "I don't think it's your fault. I think she's used to being independent and having her own space. She's not used to a busy household with people coming and going all the time."

Some of the guilt eased around Josh's heart. "And yet she loved being with us when she was little." Had loved him. It had felt good to be her hero. The one she confided in.

"Do you have feelings for her?"

Josh jarred at the question. Dad wasn't teasing. His eyes held his, seeking the truth.

Josh leaned back in the chair and sighed. "I don't know. I don't know her anymore. She makes me feel … inferior."

Dad looked thoughtful. "I don't think she means to. She's got a lot of reason to be serious."

"She had a rough childhood."

"More than you know."

His heart sank. "Why? What happened?"

Dad looked down at the open Bible on the desk in front of him. Shuffled a few books around. Then he met Josh's gaze and sighed.

"Her parents left the mission field because she was attacked."

Oh God, no.

Dad read his thoughts. "Not that way. The islanders threatened them. One had Hallie around the neck. He threatened to kill her if they didn't leave."

Josh felt all the air leave his lungs. "That's why they came back home?"

Dad nodded. "She's one tough girl. Woman."

Josh laughed. "I kind of miss that little girl she was."

Dad leaned forward on his desk. "She's still in there, Josh. You just have to work a bit harder to find her. She's still our Hallie."

Josh wasn't sure, but he hoped so.

"Just like you're still that little boy with dreams, even if you push them aside to protect yourself." Dad's expression was too knowing. "Don't be scared to dream again, Josh. Just dream with God, trusting Him to be the one to guide you and lift you if you fall."

———

"WHAT IS YOUR TREASURE? What is the most important thing to you in the whole world?" Hallie asked the group of children seated on the floor in front of the church that Sunday. It was her first time giving the children's talk in church and she was nervous.

"My BMX," one child called out.

"My PlayStation."

"My kitten."

At that one, Hallie couldn't help glancing to where Josh sat down the back of the church beside Brandon. He was looking away. Was he listening? Maybe she was being too preachy.

Seven-year-old Josiah shook his head. "Uh uh, our treasure is meant to be God. The Bible says that where your treasure is, that's where your heart lies."

For the first time Hallie realized what a pain she must have been in Sunday school. She hadn't meant to be a know-it-all, stealing the teacher's thunder. She'd assumed it was expected of her. That a good missionary's daughter would know all the answers.

"You got it," Hallie beamed at him. "How'd you know what I was going to say next?"

The congregation laughed, but it was a warm, friendly sound.

Hallie told them a story about how poor the people were on the island where her parents lived, but how happy they were because they knew and loved Jesus. Because they had eternal life.

"It's because Jesus is their treasure," she said. She pulled out her Bible. "And here is the verse Josiah told us about. Matthew six verse twenty. Josiah, can you read it out for us?"

Josiah stood, pride in his eyes as he began to read.

"Do not store up for yourselves treasures on earth, where moths and vermin destroy, and where thieves break in and steal. But store up for yourselves treasures in heaven where moths and vermin do not

destroy, and where thieves do not break in and steal. For where your treasure is, there your heart will be also."

"Where does your heart lie?" Hallie asked the children. She was aware that Josh was now watching her intently. She tried to focus on the children as she finished the story and went back to her seat.

As soon as Uncle Theo ended the service, Hallie went to the front to pack up the pictures she'd used for the children's talk.

"That's not how I would have told it."

Hallie's hand froze as she looked at Josh. She told herself not to be defensive.

"How would you have told it?"

He grinned as he helped gather the pictures. "I would have given an object lesson. Offered them each a candy that you've had stored in a box for them. Then open the box and discover it's empty because someone ate them." He pointed to himself and batted his lashes at her.

She smiled. "A thief."

"Or a moth." He grinned. "I could have dressed up as a moth and fluttered in behind you while you told the story."

She laughed. She could picture it. "Well, I'll ask you next time I'm stuck on a story idea." It actually wasn't a bad idea.

He leaned on the easel she'd set her pictures on. His expression turned thoughtful. "To be honest, I was surprised at how materialistic most of those kids are."

"It's because they have trouble thinking in the abstract," Hallie said. "Everything has to be concrete. I mean, some of them probably value the love of their parents more than anything in the world, but they can't put that into words."

He nodded. "I guess so. It's not easy for some adults either."

Hallie smiled in understanding. "So if you were to try to put it into words, where would you say your heart lies, Josh?"

He chuckled. "That's a very personal question."

She nodded. "You're right. It is. But it's an important one."

He leaned harder on the easel. "Tell you what, you tell me where your heart lies, and I'll tell you where mine lies."

Hallie didn't hesitate. "In God."

At that moment, the easel collapsed beneath Josh. Hallie went off into peals of laughter as he fell to the ground. She wasn't sure whether Josh had done it deliberately to avoid answering her question, but she decided to let it go.

Josh reached a hand up to her. "So are you going to help me up?"

"Not strong enough to get up on your own?" She blushed as she heard the flirty tone of her voice.

He tilted his head to the side. "I think you're asking for trouble, Holly."

She reached out her hand and his strong fingers wrapped around hers. She couldn't think. The warmth of his hand around hers did funny things to her heart. Then she realized his blue eyes held hers. Still looking at her, he stood up on his own. She doubted she could have pulled him up, anyway. She had to say something, anything to fill the awkwardness of the moment. She gave a shaky laugh. "I think you need to go on a diet."

He smiled. "I think you need a stronger easel."

———

ALL NIGHT JOSH thought about Hallie's question. Did he treasure God? Sure, he delivered groceries to people in need, but that had become a way of making himself feel useful. It made him feel like a good Christian. Like he was doing his bit.

He'd arranged for the church to donate to Hallie, but if he was honest, that was for his own benefit too. He wanted her to stay in Trinity Lakes. Despite her uppity ways, he liked her. She made his world a more exciting place.

If he was honest, his heart lay in his own happiness. Not even in another person or object. His treasure was himself. He shook his head in disgust. He was supposed to love God with all his heart, soul, mind and strength, but somewhere along the way Christianity had become a way of life to him, rather than a relationship with Christ Himself.

A crushing devastation filled Josh's heart. Sitting on the edge of his bed, he bent forward, his head in his hands. When was the last time he'd taken such an honest, raw examination of his life?

Maybe life wasn't as serious as Hallie made out, but it certainly deserved more respect than he gave it. God deserved more respect and love. And so did the people He created.

When had he last prayed and asked God what He'd like from him—even who he should deliver groceries to? When had he last been aware of God's presence with him? When had he last enjoyed a church service because it was an opportunity to meet with God's people and worship and learn more about Jesus rather than an opportunity to sit up the back with Brandon and make fun of people?

He knew when. Before he went to Australia. When he'd received a baseball scholarship into Grace Seminary and all his dreams were coming true.

He rubbed his burning eyes.

He'd stopped trusting God because God hadn't done what he wanted or expected. But he wanted to know Jesus again. Personally. He wanted to trust God again. To believe He really had good things for him.

Josh lifted his eyes. "God? I'm sorry. Help me trust again. Help me believe."

No other words would come, but God knew his heart. Peace filled him as he lay back down beneath the covers. He fell asleep with hope for the future for the first time in four years.

CHAPTER TEN

Hallie walked home from the Browns, her heart full. The children responded so well to her stories. Uncle Theo used to read her stories when she was a child. Sometimes she'd stayed overnight with the Ladans and Uncle Theo always read Jodie a bedtime story, snuggled up beside her on the lounge. Hallie had watched with longing until Uncle Theo invited her to sit on his other side. His arm had come around her, and she'd sat stiffly at first, but eventually the soothing sound of his voice had relaxed her, and she'd rested her head on his chest. The beat of his heart had been comforting. She'd imagined he was Jesus.

The sound of car tires pulling up beside her caused panic to well up within.

"Hallie?"

Hallie expelled a breath of relief at the sight of the town sheriff.

"I wanted to give you an update."

She came to the car window, heart pounding. His face was so serious.

"Someone we believe to be Malcolm was spotted in a stolen car in Utah. He escaped the police, but the car was found yesterday, burned out near the border to Idaho. Unfortunately that means it was impossible to get prints."

Hallie gasped. "You think he's coming after me?"

"It's possible. It's also possible that he's just on the run and happened to head this way. We'll be keeping a closer eye on your house, though. If you see anything out of place—anything —I want you to contact me. And it might be safer not to walk on your own." He waved to the passenger seat of his car. "Jump in. I'll take you home."

Hallie climbed in, trying to process what he was saying. She'd finally begun to feel safe. Now that security had all been stripped away once again.

Lord? I don't want to live in fear. Please help them catch Malcolm.

Sheriff Thompson gave her a compassionate look as he dropped her off at her cottage. "We'll catch him, Hallie."

"Thank you."

He smiled. "Hey, it's our job."

She nodded and watched as he drove off. She opened her mailbox as she did every day. She hadn't had any mail yet, but she always hoped.

An envelope. She smiled and pulled it out, flipped it over. From the church. She carefully lifted the seal, then stared at the bank check made out in her name. Her mouth dropped at the amount. She couldn't accept this.

A small piece of paper fluttered to the ground, and she bent to pick it up, hands shaking.

A gift for you from all of us at Trinity Life Church. Thank you for all you do. You are a gift from God.

That was it. Overwhelmed, Hallie drew in a deep breath. Her throat tightened and her eyes stung.

Lord? Everything in her wanted to return the gift. To reassure the church that she had enough money to stay here at least six months. Except now … She smiled, blinking back tears. She could stay longer. She could arrange for Amanda to sell her car in Missouri. She could buy a new car here. God was looking after her. Her smile widened as joy filled her heart.

Thank you, Lord. Please bless this amazing, giving church.

A loud honking noise from the Junk Man's backyard caught her attention. She walked down the driveway to look over the fence. Geese waddled around the Junk Man's feet, flapping and honking.

He gently picked up a bird with a strapped wing and inspected it. Hallie smiled. There was something about the unusual man that drew her. She was sure he was wounded, just like his geese.

She glanced at the envelope in her hand, her heart full. If God had prompted people to give to her so generously, if she believed God would help her with the Brown children, then it made sense to believe God could—would—use her to reach the Junk Man.

"Good afternoon," she called above the noise of the birds.

He glanced up, nodded, then went back to his birds. Hallie watched, intrigued, as he carefully picked up another bird and tenderly checked its splinted leg. There was a confidence and competence about him that told her he had the potential to be something more than he was.

"What happened to the bird?" she called out when the noise died down.

The Junk Man wandered over to the fence. "Fishing line." His words were clipped and his voice raspy from lack of use. Hallie caught a glimpse of anger in his tone, but it was his eyes that caught her. They were an unusual, expressive green. She'd seen him somewhere before. But where?

He shuffled his feet then looked at her with resolve. "Got any pets?"

She shook her head, appreciating his effort to carry on the conversation, even though he was obviously uncomfortable. "No, but I love cats."

He almost smiled through his rugged beard. "My least favorite," he said. "They eat my favorites." He pointed to one of the bird cages. "Cat got two of them last year."

"I'm sorry."

He shrugged. "Wasn't your cat, since you don't have one." With that, he headed back toward one of the tumble-down sheds and Hallie watched him go.

Well, she'd met him now and he wasn't so bad.

———

JOSH DROVE HOME from work feeling restless. Another day at work, and he'd just dropped a bag of groceries on the Carrigan's front porch. He'd told himself for years that he was happy with his mundane job, but he'd been afraid to want more until now. Afraid to do anything that cost him personally. Not like Dad did in his ministry. Not like Hallie when she reached out to those children. He missed the challenge of going out of his comfort zone and seeing God work in unexpected ways. Of daring to dream God had a purpose for him beyond all he'd ever imagined. A purpose of eternal significance.

He pulled into the driveway and looked up at the house. It was beautiful. Grand yet understated. And the same every single day.

Lord, what is your plan for me? He couldn't study at any college, let alone seminary. He'd need special accommodations. People would find out about his disability. He'd have to memorize his sermons. Have the computer read back anything he'd written.

But what was so wrong with that? He was disappointed that Hallie wouldn't open up to him and yet he refused to open up to her. Until he did, their friendship would remain surface deep. And that thought pained him. He wanted more. Wanted what they'd had as children.

With a sigh, he walked up the front steps. Brandon was still at work. Jodie would be, too. He needed a distraction. Would it be wrong to go and visit Hallie in her little cottage? Would she want him to?

Lord, give me the courage to tell Hallie about my condition if that's the right thing to do.

He opened the door to the sound of the landline ringing. It hardly ever rang these days. Mom peeked around the kitchen door.

"Josh, is that you? Can you get that?"

"Got it." Josh dropped his keys on the hall table and grabbed the phone.

"Hello, Josh here."

"Hello, is this the Ladan home?"

"Yes. Who am I speaking to?"

"I'm Amanda. I need to get in contact with Hallie Hollaway. It's urgent."

Josh moved into the kitchen while Mom mouthed, *Who is it?*

He shrugged. "She's not here," he said into the phone. "Can I give her a message?" He tried to analyze the woman's voice. Professional but warm. Friendly but hesitant to pass along information. A friend of Hallie's? An old work colleague?

The voice came again. "She's not answering her phone. Do you know if she's okay?"

Josh frowned. "Why wouldn't she be?"

Silence.

"Ma'am?"

"Look, I'd really appreciate it if you can ask her to give me a call as soon as possible."

"Can do. Who do I say was calling?"

The woman gave a half laugh. "Oh, of course. Amanda, her old boss." She gave another awkward half laugh. "I mean, previous boss. It's important, okay?"

"Okay." He got that. Why was the woman so flustered? And why wasn't Hallie answering her phone?

When he related the call to Mom, she waved the pot mitt she was holding at him. "Why don't you go and see if she's home? Give her the message. Oh, and ask if she wants to come for dinner."

Josh nodded and scooped his keys back up, glad to have an excuse to check on Hallie. And to see her again.

He was relieved when she answered his first knock on the cottage door.

"Josh. I didn't expect to see you."

He leaned an arm against the frame and grinned cheekily. "Oh, but aren't you glad you have?"

She almost smiled. "I reserve my judgment for the time being."

He looked closer at her. Had she been crying? "Is everything okay?"

She nodded. "All good. Want to come in?"

"Sure." He followed her into the tiny living room where she sat and pointed to another chair. He studied her more closely. "You've been crying."

She instantly turned red.

He sat down. "So everything isn't okay."

His heart tightened when tears filled her eyes. "I'm just overwhelmed. At God's goodness." She gave him a watery smile. "God has provided my every need."

Oh. So she'd received the check from the church. He smiled, then tried to stop himself.

He pointed to her phone. "A friend of yours called our landline. Amanda? She was worried because you weren't answering."

Hallie frowned and picked up her phone, then smiled. "Oh. I forgot I put it on silent while I was teaching."

"Amanda seemed worried something might have happened to you."

Hallie rolled her eyes. "She's like a mother hen."

He smiled, thinking Hallie could do with a mother figure like that. Speaking of which … "Mom wants to know if you'd like to come for dinner. But maybe you should call your mother hen first."

Hallie drew in a deep breath. "I'd love to come to dinner, but I don't know if I'll be very good company. I'm really tired. Playing with kids is harder than I expected."

He chuckled. "Now the truth comes out. You don't work at all. You just play."

She screwed up her nose. "Yeah, but playing is hard work when it doesn't come naturally."

Was she having a go at him? Making a point? She didn't seem to be. He studied her a moment longer. Her darker hair was growing on him.

"I could pick you up and drop you home if that helps." Her eyes widened. What had he said? "To save you some energy."

She studied him out of those big blue eyes, as if searching for something. He wished he knew what. She must have found it because she smiled. "Thank you. I'd appreciate that. I'm thinking it's time to sell my car in Springfield and buy one here. Do you know anyone selling?"

"No, but Brandon would. You could ask him."

The light in her eyes dimmed. She stood. "Okay. Well, thanks for stopping by. I'll see you tonight."

He took the hint and stood, too. "I look forward to it. I'll be back to pick you up at six."

Obviously now hadn't been the right time to tell her about his condition. Relief and disappointment warred within him as he left.

Lord, help me to trust your timing.

————

HALLIE WAITED until Josh's car turned the corner before she called Amanda.

"Hallie? Is that you?" Amanda sounded panicky.

Hallie laughed. "Well, it's not Malcolm."

"Don't joke about it. I've been trying to call you for hours."

"I had my phone on silent. Sorry about that."

"Has the sheriff talked to you?"

"Yes. I was going to call you. He suggested I shouldn't walk around town by myself, so I wondered how you'd feel about selling my car for me? I'll buy another one here."

"That's a good idea." Amanda sounded relieved. "It should sell easily. It's a great little car."

"I'll pay you for your time and effort."

Amanda laughed. "No, you won't. I hate not being able to do anything to help, but … well, this is something I can do."

"Thanks, Manda."

"Promise me you'll be careful?"

"Of course." Hallie could hear the worry in her friend's voice. "Thanks for looking out for me, but I'm okay. I promise. God is looking after me."

She told her about the check she'd received from the church, about a friend offering to drive her around, and about the friendship and support of Uncle Theo, Aunty Lil, and Jodie.

"So they're like family to you?"

Hallie smiled. "Yes. Like you are. God has been good to me."

"Sounds like it. Who was the young man who answered the phone when I called their house?"

"That was Josh Ladan."

"You didn't mention him. How old is he?" Amanda sounded amused.

"Manda."

"What? I'm just asking. Although it speaks volumes that you didn't mention him. Silence can speak louder than words."

Hallie blew out a breath. "He's not … I don't know if I can trust him."

Amanda said nothing.

"You still there?"

"I'm here. Hallie, don't let what Malcolm did take away your ability to trust. To love."

Hallie bit her lip. Was that what she was doing? A memory she'd forgotten filtered back and she found herself choked up. Uncle Theo had been away at a seminar, and Jodie had asked Josh to read to them before bed. He'd agreed. And she and Jodie had sat on either side of him, snuggled against him, as he read. He'd used funny voices and they'd both ended up giggling and hyped until Aunty Lil scolded Josh.

"You're supposed to be helping them settle," she'd said. He'd grinned but toned it down.

Hallie remembered the way he'd given her and Jodie a good night hug afterwards. For a child starved of affection and friendship, it had warmed her heart. A picture of her hugging the man Josh filled her mind and her face heated. So not the same.

"Hallie? You there?"

Hallie came back to the present with a thump. "Yeah, sorry. Just tired. I might have a power nap before going over to the Ladans' for dinner."

"Okay. Thank them from me for looking out for you." She chuckled. "And give Josh your love for me."

It took Hallie a moment to process what she'd said. "Amanda!"

She ended the call to the sound of Amanda's laughter.

CHAPTER ELEVEN

Hallie told herself to stop being ridiculous when Josh arrived to pick her up and her heart started fluttering like a schoolgirl with a crush. She was just overtired and emotional. A power nap had been out of the question once she'd stirred up her childhood memories of Josh.

He studied her as she clicked her seatbelt into place. "You okay?"

She nodded, unable to look at him when he had that caring, concerned expression on his face. And when his muscles flexed on the steering wheel that way. She fought the image of herself hugging him. Feeling the soft cotton of his shirt against her cheek, and his firm chest beneath it.

Stop it. "I'm okay." Except she wasn't. She shut her eyes. "Just tired."

Just? There was so much more going on, but she'd work out how to regain self-control. God would help her capture every thought and guard her heart. She'd trust Him to do it.

Please Lord, because I'm not having much success in my own strength.

Josh didn't speak the rest of the drive, and she knew he was allowing her to rest.

Jodie wasn't so accommodating. She met Hallie at the door, bouncing with enthusiasm.

"Hallie, I've got a big favor to ask from you."

Josh frowned. "Let her get inside first."

Jodie grinned and pushed Hallie gently toward the living room. "Quick, sit down."

Hallie couldn't help smiling at Jodie. "What is it?"

"There's this woman at work who has a little girl, Madison. She needs someone to care for her after school but can't afford to pay anyone. She's a single mom. It would only be a few hours." Jodie's voice was rushed as though she was scared Hallie would say no. Her voice turned soft. "At the moment, the poor little girl arrives home from school on the bus and has to go inside and lock the door and stay there 'til her mom gets home."

Hallie gasped. "Is that even legal?"

"She's got no other option. And the poor kid got freaked out when a delivery man rang the bell and hung around on the front porch for a few minutes. Called her mom in tears."

Hallie's chest tightened. That poor little girl. Fear was awful. Being alone and afraid was even worse. Was this another opportunity to give a child a childhood she was missing?

"I'll do it. I don't have a car yet though. How will she get to my place?"

"I'm sure we'll work something out." Jodie's voice went soft. "Thank you, Hallie. I love how God provides. He brought you all the way from Missouri to help out my friend Cassie."

Hallie smiled. Yes, for that reason, and so many more.

But Josh was frowning. "You're over here for a break, but all you do is work. Taking on another child is a huge responsibility."

"I know. But if I don't have Madison, I'll just be reading on my own at home or going for a walk or hassling you guys with another visit."

"Nothing wrong with that."

Hallie looked at him. He didn't know she wasn't safe walking around town anymore.

"You won't have any time to even think with a little girl tagging along after you all day."

She smiled. Almost said, *Like I did with you?* and stopped herself in time. "It's not all day. It's only in the afternoon. And this is an opportunity to give her the childhood she deserves. To have fun with her. To teach her how valuable she is to God. No child should be stuck at home, door locked, alone, afraid. The love of Jesus costs. He gave his life for me, so it's a small thing to give up a bit of spare time for a child He loves."

Josh studied her thoughtfully, then shook his head. "You're old beyond your years, aren't you? Sometimes I feel like you're my mother."

Hallie's heart sank. She didn't mean to come across that way. She didn't want Josh to feel like she was correcting and rebuking him.

As he walked away, his phone rang. Hallie watched, troubled. But he was back only moments later, grinning from ear to ear.

"Just had a fight with Sarah."

Sarah? What had happened with Rachel? Had Josh ever had a girlfriend who lasted more than a week?

Jodie groaned. "So what's new? She'll be back to apologize in the morning."

"I doubt she'll be back," Josh didn't seem concerned about it.

"What makes you so sure?"

He chuckled. "She's not very happy."

Jodie frowned. "What did you do, Josh?"

"All I did was offered to buy her a pair of glasses. She said she can't see me anymore so I said I'd buy her glasses. Problem solved."

Hallie tried to hold back her smile. It was so childish it was funny. But Josh seemed to have no idea how deeply he affected these girls. He was here, smiling and joking, while Sarah was probably crying her eyes out because she finally realized Josh was never going to love her the way she loved him.

Josh was so likable, and yet so many things about him bothered her. He didn't act the way a committed Christian should act. Sometimes his faith appeared to be a half-hearted act used for his own purposes.

Lord, soften his heart, she prayed. *But don't break it too badly in the process.*

Hallie's heart was light as she arrived at the Browns' home the following morning. She smiled cheerfully at Eden and Abella, then looked over at Jimmy playing on the floor.

"Good morning, Jimmy."

Eden shook her head. "He won't answer to Jimmy anymore. He's Batman. You have to call him Batman or he won't answer."

Hallie's eyes widened. "Seriously?"

Eden nodded. "For real. Mom had to call him Batman, so he'd eat his breakfast this morning."

Hallie wondered if she could bring herself to call the little boy Batman. But she needed to communicate with him. It wouldn't hurt her to play his game, to allow him his childhood.

"Okay, Batman, will you sit over here with me?"

Immediately, "Batman" complied, and Hallie chuckled. Yet his pseudo character bothered her. When Jimmy grew into a young man would he believe it was okay to assume another name to suit his own fantasies and gain a girl? She would come up with a Bible story to tell them about the importance of honesty.

Or was that her own fear talking? How could she share

Jesus's love when she kept getting in the way? When her past and her fears clouded her thinking?

Lord, help me please. I really want to love these children the way you do. Selflessly. Sacrificially.

HALLIE KEPT her eyes open as she walked home that afternoon.

Please God, keep me safe.

Her heart jumped at the sight of an unfamiliar car parked out the front of her cottage. Then she laughed at herself. It would be Madison and her mother. If only the police would catch Malcolm, then she could stop expecting him to be around every corner.

Madison and her mother were already inside the cottage front gate, inspecting the garden. Hallie smiled as the poor mother tried to curb her little girl's enthusiasm.

"Look Mommy, that one's like in your garden. Isn't it?" Madison bounced up and down while her mother pulled her hand back from the white flower. Hallie didn't even know what it was.

"Yes darling, that's a rhododendron. Don't touch though. They bruise easily."

The little girl looked up and let out a cry of delight, rushing to the gate to meet Hallie.

"Are you my new babysitter? Mom said it's not really babysitting 'cause I'm not a baby. We'll just have fun together."

Hallie smiled at the little girl whose soft brown hair hung in waves around her adorable heart-shaped face. Her hazel eyes sparkled with joy. Perhaps Madison didn't need her so much as she needed Madison.

"Yes, that's me." Hallie looked to the girl's mother who smiled.

"I'm Cassie. Thank you so much for this. Jodie spoke so highly of you I knew I could trust you with my little girl."

Hallie smiled, and her heart warmed. "It will be a delight to have her, Cassie."

A small hand slipped into hers. Madison gazed up at her with a huge smile.

"Can we do drawing?"

"Of course. Want to say goodbye to your mom first?"

Madison threw her arms around her mother, who smiled down at her affectionately and placed a kiss on her cheek.

"Be good, Maddie."

"Always." Madison blew her a kiss, then focused on Hallie's front door. "Can we draw now?"

Hallie laughed. "Yes."

The problem was pens didn't quite do the job. And she didn't have any pencils or crayons. She wasn't willing to risk taking Madison for a walk to the shops. All she could think to do was call Josh, who was happy to oblige.

Josh soon arrived with a pack of pencils, crayons, and a wide grin.

"Can I draw too?" he asked Madison.

She beamed at him. "Yes."

Josh's first picture was a stick figure drawing of Hallie driving on the right side of the road in Australia and hitting a kangaroo.

"See, kangaroos know to be on the right side of the road, but Hallie was on the wrong side."

"The left is wrong," Hallie said.

Josh shook his head. "You can't just assume that if it's not right, it's wrong."

Madison giggled.

"Poor kangaroo is now dead," Josh said in a droll tone. "Here's its head bouncing across the road."

"Josh," Hallie chastised.

But Madison was giggling harder. "I know kangaroos bounce, but not their heads, Josh."

Hallie tried to hide her reluctant smile. She stood to get a cloth and clear some of the pencil shavings Josh had left on the table. He had a way with children. Why that was so important to her, she didn't know.

"She's not really thirty, you know," Josh told Madison, pointing at Hallie. "So you can call her Holly, like I do."

Madison looked doubtful for a minute. "How old is she?"

Hallie tried to glare, but Josh's grin was too infectious. "She's forty."

Madison's eyes widened before she realized Josh was messing with her.

"So you can call her Grandma if you don't want to call her Holly," Josh said.

Hallie avoided his eyes as she collected the cloth and moved toward the table.

"How many grandkids do you have, Holly?" Josh asked, clearly trying to provoke a response.

Hallie tried to pass him, sink cloth in her hand, but he moved his chair back, pinning her against the wall.

"I'm not married." She attempted to shove him out of the way.

"Do you want to be?"

Hallie ignored him, but Maddison's eyes lit up. "Do you have a boyfriend Miss …" she glanced at Josh before turning back to Hallie. "Holly?"

"No."

"Josh can be your boyfriend."

Madison's tone was full of enthusiasm, but Hallie shook her head, still avoiding Josh's eyes. "Josh already has too many girl-friends. And if I'm forty, I'm too old to be one of them. Now, Josh, will you please let this poor old woman pass …"

With a carefree grin, Josh moved his chair back in to let her pass.

"Madison, do you think you could do something for me?"

His whisper was intentionally loud enough for Hallie to hear. "Do you think you could make Holly feel young again? Make her laugh and smile?"

Madison nodded seriously.

"Make her act like she's a teenager again."

Madison's eyes widened as she looked to Hallie. "Are you only a teenager?"

"No, I'm actually twenty-one." Hallie forced herself to smile. Josh was teasing her, yet his words hurt. He really thought she acted like a serious old woman. When she was young, Josh had never seemed to mind her above-average intelligence. In fact, he'd seemed to respect and admire her for it. But something had changed over the years. She wasn't sure if it was her or if it was Josh.

Josh had left by the time Cassie came to collect Madison. The joy on the little girl's face lifted Hallie's heart. Madison bounced up and down so hard she lost all the pictures she held out to show her mother. With a smile, Hallie bent to pick them up. Thankfully the pictures Madison held were tame. She'd taken Josh's picture of the bouncing kangaroo head out, saying she wanted to keep it herself.

It disgusted her to admit that was the truth.

THE HOUSE WAS quiet without Madison and Josh. Hallie went to sit out on the back step. She could see the mountains in the distance. The cooler temperatures indicated they would soon be covered in snow. The maple leaves in the Junk Man's yard were already turning a golden yellow. The Junk Man was standing beneath the tree, strapping the wing of a bird. Hallie came to the fence.

"What kind of bird is it?"

The Junk Man looked up. "This one's a ring-necked duck. Got hit by a car."

"Will it be okay?"

The Junk Man continued his work. "If I have anything to say about it, yes. She's a bit too quiet for my liking though. I'll keep her inside in the warm until she perks up."

Hallie smiled. "It does get noisy over here sometimes."

The Junk Man's head jerked up, brows lowering over his expressive eyes. "It bother you?"

"No. Oh no. It gets too quiet in this little cottage by myself."

He grunted. "You need to find yourself a nice young man to marry."

Hallie laughed. What was with the marriage theme today? "I don't know if that would be any better."

"Me neither." He picked up the duck and tucked it under his arm where it buried its head in the crease of his elbow. "Can't trust people enough to ever get close enough to marry." He looked down at the duck and Hallie thought he smiled, though it was hard to tell through his beard. "These creatures ... you can trust them. They always listen. They never judge. They don't compete with you. They'll never betray you or pretend to be something they're not."

Hallie blinked. What was the Junk Man's story? Who had betrayed him? She had a sudden, strong urge to know him. To know his story.

"I'm Hallie," she said, realizing she hadn't introduced herself.

He looked at her, eyes appraising, as though he were looking into her soul. "My real friends have always called me Mac."

"I'd like to be one of your real friends."

There was no mistaking his smile this time. "Then feel free to call me Mac. I'll tell you if I want you to stop."

Hallie drew in a deep breath, looking directly into those deep eyes of his. "I hope that never happens."

His smile disappeared. He grunted and turned away. "We'll see." He opened his back door and went inside.

CHAPTER TWELVE

"Heard you've been visiting Frog Swamp a bit lately," Brandon said as he straightened the net on the Ladans' Ping-Pong table.

Josh studied him. What was Brandon's point? "Just helping a friend."

Brandon stepped back and picked up his paddle. "Don't know how you can be friends with someone who hardly talks. She looks down her nose at everyone. Acts like a princess ruling her kingdom, making sure everyone's doing the right thing."

Josh frowned. He didn't mind Brandon criticizing people, even joined in sometimes, but it was different now he was criticizing Hallie. Sure, Hallie could make a person feel inferior, but she deserved respect.

"Maybe you need to give her a chance. Actually get to know her."

Brandon grinned. "See if I can melt the ice queen? Sounds like a challenge."

Josh's hand tightened on his paddle.

Brandon studied him thoughtfully. "Something you're not telling me?"

Josh blinked. Time to deflect. Pretend to misunderstand his question. "She's more than she seems, that's all." He remembered what Dad had told him about her being attacked on the mission field. "And yes, I do know things about her you don't, but they're not my secrets to tell."

Brandon looked hurt and Josh felt bad. Usually they didn't keep any secrets from one another. That's what made them so close.

He sighed. "You might actually like her if you made the effort to get to know her."

Brandon huffed. "Looks like I'd better since you've decided she's family."

Family. He'd insisted she wasn't family, but he had to admit he'd brought her into that circle. Loyalty was important to Josh and Brandon. They both knew not to criticize one another's family. Everyone else was fair game.

"She kind of is," Josh said. "She basically lived here when she was younger."

Brandon's expression changed. "Why?"

"She was an only child. Her parents were ..." He stopped. Could he trust Brandon to respect what he told him about Hallie? It bothered him that he couldn't. "Look, I just wish you'd make an effort to get to know her. I was hoping you'd help her out."

Brandon reached for a Ping-Pong ball. "Yeah? How?"

"She wants to buy a car. I thought you might know someone wanting to sell."

"Does she even have a license?"

"Yes. She's very independent and capable. She left her car in Missouri. That's all."

Brandon looked thoughtful. "Did you ever find out why she left?"

"No."

Brandon laughed. "You're challenging me to get to know her when you don't know what happened in Missouri?"

It was true. But he hadn't told her about his disability either. Maybe if he did, she would open up more.

Brandon pulled back his paddle to serve and stopped as Jodie walked into the room.

"Hey guys. Who's winning?"

Brandon smirked. "Me. I always win. At games. At life. At love."

Jodie let out an unladylike snort. "Says who?"

Josh grinned. That was his sister.

Brandon placed a hand over his heart. "Says my heart."

"I think your heart deceives you."

Brandon looked over at Josh. "We'll see."

Josh tried to work out what his friend was thinking. He knew that look. Once it had meant Brandon was cooking up some kind of crazy scheme. It meant fun and excitement. Now it made him nervous.

"You know what's wrong with you guys?" Jodie picked up a paddle, clearly assuming she was going to play the winner.

Brandon smirked and ruffled her hair. "Nothing, but I'm sure your heart will deceive you and come up with something."

Jodie pulled away from him. "You think females are transparent. You think you know exactly what we're thinking. Like you have this secret passage into their hearts where you can devour all their secrets and then play the secrets of their hearts against them."

Wow. Josh blinked. Jodie didn't mince words. Had she heard their earlier conversation?

Jodie poked her paddle in Brandon's face. He pushed hers away and moved his paddle up to make a serve. She leaned against the table so he couldn't make a shot, glaring up at him.

"You might know a lot about people, but you have no respect

for that knowledge. And that's scary. Yeah, you can be funny, but you're also insensitive. Jesus accepted the outcasts and sinners. He didn't make fun of them and rub their noses in the dirt."

She was right. She had Brandon pinned. But was Josh much better? The realization stung. He'd seen the look of hurt and confusion on Sarah's face when she spotted him in the supermarket. She'd turned and quickly walked the other way. If anyone treated Esther or Jodie the way he'd treated her ... Or Hallie, for that matter.

He hadn't heard the rest of what Jodie and Brandon were saying, but Jodie looked furious. She spun around, dumped her paddle down and left the room.

Brandon wiped his forehead. "Phew. I thought she was going to have us for dinner."

Josh said nothing, but he wished he had the courage to tell Brandon Jodie had made some excellent points.

"I've got a challenge to win now." Brandon waved his paddle in the air, pinning Josh with his gaze. "I will get to know the ice queen and melt her heart. She will pour her secrets out to me and trust me with her life. If you win this game, I might consider sharing them with you."

Brandon slammed the ball across the net and Josh's focus was taken up making sure he returned Brandon's serve. And yet something at the back of his mind told him he should be taking more notice of Brandon's words and the meaning behind them.

"HELLO, BRANDON." Hallie was surprised to see him standing at the door to the Sunday school room as she finished wiping down the paint-covered tables. The children had all left to show their parents their craft works. It had been a joy to share God's heart with them, His heart for the children.

Brandon gave her an easy smile. "How's it going?"

"Good. We just finished David and Goliath. I tried to leave out the gory details, but Josiah knew them and insisted on filling us in."

Brandon laughed. "That little boy thinks he knows more than anyone else, and he wants everyone to know it. Once he tried to tell me the way a car engine really works. I put him in his place."

He was smiling, but his tone bothered Hallie. Would he have been one of those putting her in her place when she was a child? Why was he here? He picked up a drawing one of the children had left behind.

"Do you teach them a different story each time?"

Surprised by his interest, Hallie nodded. "I'll try to cover most of the well-known Bible stories first, then maybe we'll put them all in order—give them an idea how the Bible fits together."

Brandon looked sheepish. "I need to learn a bit about that." He looked so uncomfortable she decided to change the topic.

"How's work going?"

"Yeah, good. Actually, I wanted to talk to you about something." He sat on the corner of one of the tables and fiddled with a paintbrush. "Josh mentioned you're looking for a car. I don't know of any locally, but I'm keeping an eye out. The other option is I could take you to Walla Walla or Spokane to go car hunting. I know what to look for." He looked at the pile of Sunday school books in her hands. "In the meantime, I can drive you where you need to go. The weather's getting too unpredictable to be walking every day."

Hallie frowned. Why was he being so nice? "I can't ask that of you." His offer felt over the top.

"Why not? We're pretty much family, you and I. Both adopted into the Ladan clan. We Ladans look out for each other."

"But you have work."

"I do enough overtime. The boss is flexible and won't mind me ducking out to help a friend."

A friend. Family. Her heart leapt in joy. Could he really be a good friend? Like he was with Josh and Jodie? She searched his face, felt a sense of déjà vu as she looked into his green eyes. Earnest, hopeful. It was unfair to be so suspicious of him. She couldn't let Malcolm's betrayal affect her that way.

She felt a smile coming. "Well, if you put it that way ..."

He grinned. "You accept?"

"Only if you promise not to copy my laugh."

He held out his hand for her to shake. "Deal."

"What's the deal?" Josh came into the room.

Brandon gave him a smug smile. "I'm taking her car hunting." He looked back at Hallie. "How about we head to Walla Walla now? I know a car yard open seven days. We can have a look and then grab a late lunch."

Hallie's heart lifted. God truly was providing all her needs. She hadn't even needed to explain to anyone why she no longer wanted to walk places alone. She'd been looking over her shoulder every step of the way to church this morning.

"Thank you so, so much. You're a gift from God."

He laughed and batted his eyelashes. "That's what all the women say."

Fire lit her face. "That's not what I meant."

He grinned. "Perhaps I'll have to make you mean it." He looked over at Josh and gave him a triumphant smile that set Hallie on edge. She pushed the feeling aside. Malcolm had made her paranoid. Trusting was hard, but she needed to leave the past in the past and let Brandon be a friend if he wanted to be.

He opened his pickup door for her. "Get in and I'll show you how a real truck drives."

She laughed and he grinned.

"I mean it. Manuals like this are getting harder to buy, which is a tragedy. There's nothing like being able to change the gears yourself, being in tune with the engine, feeling the power, working with her."

Hallie laughed. "Did you just call your truck *her?*"

"Not saying." He revved the engine and made his way out of town. Although smooth, his driving was fast. Hallie couldn't see the speedometer from where she sat, but she suspected he was over the limit.

He swerved around an oncoming vehicle, narrowly missing a tree and she managed to hold in a gasp. He was capable and had good reflexes, but she was concerned for the other driver. She hoped they hadn't had a heart attack from the fright.

CHAPTER THIRTEEN

Josh lay on his bed, a cool cloth over his forehead. Stupid migraine. Just when he needed his wits about him. What was Brandon up to? Was he helping Hallie because he cared enough to get to know her, or was this all a game, a challenge to him? Hallie acted together and mature, but she needed to be treated tenderly so old wounds weren't ripped open.

"Nice escape." Jodie's teasing lilt came through the partially open door.

He almost smiled. "I know why you think I'm pretending, and I don't blame you." Kyla had come for lunch. Had told Dad she needed to speak with him about some issues with his sermon. Rather than suggest she find another church, he'd graciously invited her to lunch to discuss it.

"So you really do have a migraine?"

He nodded.

"You okay?" She sounded genuinely concerned now.

He opened his eyes, squinting against the light. "I don't know."

"Hey, what happened?" The bed shifted as she sat on the edge.

"Brandon's taking Hallie car hunting."

Surprise crossed her features. "Why?"

"He wants to get to know her better."

"Why?"

It was a fair enough question. Brandon had never shown any interest in being Hallie's friend before now. He bit his lip. "He wanted to know about her past and I wouldn't tell him. I told him to find out for himself. I didn't mean for it to come out sounding like a challenge, but ..."

Jodie's face registered shock then horror. "Is that what you were talking about that day I came in, when you were playing table tennis?"

"Yeah."

"Oh no." Her eyes slid shut. "And then I made it worse, going off at him like that. He's stubborn. The more you tell him not to do something, the more he's likely to do it."

"I know." The pain in his head intensified and nausea churned his stomach.

Jodie looked like she was going to cry. "What did you actually say to him?"

"I don't remember exactly. But he called her an ice queen. Said he'd melt her heart and find out her secrets before I did." Josh pinched the bridge of his nose. What had he done?

Jodie's chin wobbled. "He wouldn't, would he? Play with Hallie's heart just to get information out of her?"

Yes. Yes, he would. For the first time, his and Brandon's hearts were completely at odds. The way they should have been a long time ago. When had he started thinking it was okay to treat people like objects? Brandon was the new Christian. Josh should have been influencing Brandon, not the other way around.

"What are we going to do?" Jodie clasped her hands together. "We can't have him playing with her heart like that."

A gasp came from the doorway. "You're going to tell her, that's what."

Kyla. Josh's heart sank further. *God help us.*

Kyla stood in the doorway glaring at them, dark eyes glittering. "The Bible says to confess your sins to one another. If you're truly sorry, you need to repent and confess what you've done."

Josh wished he had the energy to sit up, but Jodie was already standing. "What are you doing up here?" Her voice was cold.

Kyla tapped a foot. "I could ask the same thing. Your mother is down there slaving away in the kitchen and you two are up here doing nothing."

"Where's Dad?"

"He had to take a call in his office."

"That doesn't give you any right to come up here, in a private home and eavesdrop on a private conversation." Her voice rose as she spoke.

Josh groaned and held his head. Jodie looked back at him and lowered her voice. "Sorry."

Kyla lifted her chin. "It was providential I came in here." She looked at Josh. "You're a pastor's son. You're supposed to set an example. I can't believe you'd have a bet with your friend to see who can get a girl first. What would your father say?"

Josh groaned again. This time because of the pain in his heart, not his head.

Jodie's hands went to her hips. "Kyla, you don't have the full story."

"Then explain it to me, because from what I heard, that's exactly what's going on."

"I don't think that's best."

"Allowing your brother to continue with this is what's wrong. If you don't tell Hallie what's going on, I will." Kyla turned on her heel. "Now Jodie-Lee, are you coming to help your mother, or do I need to do it?"

Jodie's eyes bored a hole in Kyla's back. She glanced at Josh. "I'll go down and see what damage control I can manage. I'll keep you updated."

Josh watched her go. How did Kyla even know Jodie's full name? None of them used it. Kyla knew way too much about everything but filtered it all through the lens of her own limited understanding.

Just like him and Brandon.

———

HALLIE SMILED at Brandon as he pulled up outside her cottage. They hadn't found a car, but Brandon had been good company. She could see why Josh liked him. He could be charming when he chose to be. She didn't know why he'd changed his attitude toward her, but she was grateful.

"Made you want a truck like mine, didn't I?" he said with a grin. His eyes were bright and alive.

She smiled. "No. But I appreciate you taking the time to help me. I don't know how to thank you."

He studied her, his green eyes searching hers. "Maybe you could trust me? Let me in on what actually goes on in your head and heart."

She laughed. "What do you want to know?"

He pulled a face. "Hmm, maybe what your childhood was like? What made you leave a perfectly good job in Missouri and come all the way here?"

Hallie blinked and pulled back. "What do you mean?"

He smiled and reached for her hand, running his work roughened fingers over hers. "I don't know. You just have this look about you. Like you're holding some deep secret. Like there's a depth to you that no one can reach until they gain your trust. Your complete trust. I guess I hope I'm one of … one of the lucky ones."

She pulled her hand from his. Did he know about Malcolm? Was he trying to play with her heart too? Or had Josh told him about her past? She blinked. Of course he had. Josh told Brandon everything. Nothing was sacred.

"What did Josh tell you?" Her voice came out high pitched. Nervous.

Brandon looked genuinely surprised. He frowned. "Nothing. Except that you're a genius who lived at the Bible college when your parents were studying. That's it." He took her hand again. "I promise."

She looked into his eyes and believed him. She blew out a breath.

"Sorry. I just thought …"

"Hey." Brandon placed a hand on her cheek, turning her face toward him. "Josh might be an idiot sometimes, but he respects you."

Did he? How she wanted to believe that. How she wished it was Josh sitting here with her, looking at her as though he really cared for her, wanted to know the deepest part of her. But she wasn't going to tell anyone about Malcolm. Some shame was too big to share.

Josh closed his eyes, wishing he could sleep off this migraine, but his mind wouldn't settle. Jodie reported that Kyla had told Dad all the things he could improve about his sermon over lunch. It didn't seem to matter that Dad was a Bible college lecturer who had been preaching for almost thirty years. Of course Dad had been gracious, Jodie had said, but he'd also agreed with Kyla that maybe their church wasn't right for her.

She hadn't told Dad about what she'd heard upstairs. Josh

almost wished she had. Having Dad involved would be a relief. He remembered Dad saying years ago that when we felt most distant from God is when we most need to talk to Him. Well, guilt had Josh feeling so isolated he couldn't bear it.

Lord?

Then he remembered some words from the Psalms.

As the deer pants for the water, so my soul longs after you.

That's how he felt. Desperate for God. Like a thirsty deer. He pulled out his phone, winced at the glare of the screen and turned it down. Where was his Bible app? He hadn't listened to it for a long time. What were those verses Kyla had mentioned? About confessing sins?

He asked his phone to find them for him. His phone's automated assistant reported the findings of James 5:16. He asked for it to be read aloud.

He listened as a deep, calming voice read the verses.

Therefore confess your sins to each other and pray for each other so that you may be healed. The prayer of a righteous person is powerful and effective.

A righteous man? Prayers?

Josh bowed his head. *Oh Lord, I'm not righteous. Nothing I do is powerful and effective. I need you. Brandon needs you. Help me know how to talk to him please. And Hallie. Please, please help Hallie. And Lord, forgive me for being so thoughtless. So selfish. Teach me how to live for you. Like Hallie does.*

JOSH WATCHED as Brandon walked into their living room the following morning and looked warily at Jodie. She'd told him they needed to see him urgently after he dropped Hallie off to work.

"What's going on?" Brandon sat down.

Arms folded tight over her chest, Jodie didn't hesitate. "I can't believe you'd treat Hallie like that."

Brandon's eyes widened. "What have I done?"

"Treated her like a challenge. Decided to be nice to her to discover her secrets."

Brandon glanced at Josh, then he sat back with a half grin. "Hey, don't stress. She wouldn't tell me anything."

Josh frowned. "I never meant it at as a challenge, Brandon. I'd never want you to be nice to her if you don't really like or respect her."

Brandon had the grace to look ashamed. "Fine. I'll back out, tell her I'm too busy to help her out or something."

Jodie let out a grunt of disgust. "Lying's not going to fix the problem. Two wrongs don't make a right."

"You really aren't interested in getting to know her? This really was just a challenge to you?" Josh felt sick.

Brandon didn't answer and Josh knew it was.

Jodie glared at Brandon, fire in her eyes. "It's too late."

"What do you mean?" Now Brandon looked alarmed.

Josh drew in a deep breath. "Kyla heard us talking yesterday."

"Heard who talking? About what?"

"I was worried about you going off with Hallie. I told Jodie about it. Kyla was listening in. She said if we don't tell Hallie what's going on, she will."

Brandon swore. Josh winced. He hadn't heard Brandon swear in a long time. Even with his mom using those words as punctuation in everyday talk, he managed to keep his language clean.

He looked at Josh, green eyes desperate. "Do you think we can talk Kyla out of it?"

"Not a chance."

They all sat in silence.

Lord, please fix this. I know we don't deserve it, but Hallie does.

Finally Brandon sighed. "Better it comes from us than her."

Josh agreed.

Jodie's eyes filled with tears. "It's going to hurt her either way." She rubbed her eyes. "Do you want me to come?"

Josh shook his head. "No, Jodes, you didn't do anything wrong. Just be praying for us? For Hallie?"

Brandon's eyes were closed, his face ashen. He stood like an old man. "I'd better get to work." He looked at Josh. "I'm supposed to pick Hallie up at three and take her home. Then she has that other little girl come over."

"I'll take her home," Jodie said. "I'll tell her you had something come up." She gave Brandon a look. "Which is true. And I'll tell Kyla you're going to speak to Hallie this evening, so she doesn't go barging in there with her own version of events."

Josh nodded and looked at Brandon. Brandon nodded too.

Jodie bit her lip and her eyes welled again. "I'll be praying for you all. God can turn anything around for good, you know. We just have to be willing to hand it to Him and trust Him."

CHAPTER FOURTEEN

Hallie sharpened the pencils Madison had left lying on the table. She was grateful Jodie had brought her home when Brandon couldn't. Jodie hadn't been herself though. She was quiet. Troubled.

Lord, please help Jodie with whatever's troubling her.

A knock came at her door. She put down the pencil and sharpener and went to open it.

"Brandon. Josh." She smiled. Neither returned it. What were they doing here?

"Are you going to ask us in?" Josh asked, his eyes connecting with hers and holding.

She blushed. "Yes. Sorry. Come in." She hurriedly straightened a few items on her table and transferred her lesson material from the sofa to the floor. Both Josh and Brandon looked around as they sat, and Hallie followed their gaze to the walls displaying pictures of cats.

Josh smiled but it wasn't as bright as normal. "You still like cats."

"What makes you think that?" She smiled back despite feeling like something was wrong.

"Where'd you get the pictures?" Josh asked.

"At the markets by the lake. I went with the Browns, and they bought them for me." She'd been grateful for the pictures. They brightened her home, helped her feel less alone.

Brandon cleared his throat. He shuffled his feet back and forth, crossing and uncrossing them. She tried to meet his eyes, wondering at the change. He and Josh were clearly uncomfortable. There was no friendly ease, no teasing, no flirting.

Josh leaned forward. "We have something we need to tell you."

Her heart skipped a beat. Had they found Malcolm? Was Jodie okay? What if Aunty Lil was sick?

"We've done something we're not proud of."

She glanced to Brandon, then back to Josh. Brandon still wouldn't look at her.

"I said something to Brandon. It was meant to be a throwaway line, but it came out as a challenge." Josh looked at Brandon.

Brandon cleared his throat again. "I ... well, I decided to help you find a car because ... well ... I deliberately tried to make you fall for me. Just to see ... if it was possible. And to see if you would tell me stuff ..."

Hallie stared at him, her mind racing. What was he saying? She looked to Josh, then waited for him to look at her. Regret shone from his eyes.

"So you were trying to manipulate me?" She knew it came out accusing, but she couldn't help it. "You don't really want to be my friend?" Brandon's look of shame confirmed it. Pain and rejection knifed her heart. "I should have known." She shook her head. "I'm so stupid. What's wrong with me? You only notice people to make fun of them or notice their weakness and make them display it as often as possible for your amusement. Why did I think it would be any different with me?"

Josh's eyes widened at her stinging allegations, but she knew he couldn't deny them.

Brandon looked truly devastated. "I'm sorry, Hallie."

Hallie shook her head. She looked at Josh, blinking back tears. "You and your throwaway lines." She bit her lip to hold back tears. "I suppose you both mimicked me, laughed at me like you do every other girl."

Josh jerked forward. "No, Holly, no—"

She cut him off. "You realize the kindest thing would have been to never tell me? If you hadn't said anything, I could have at least had the comfort of believing you really were my friends for a while ..."

"Hallie—"

"So why did you tell me?" She wasn't going to allow him any more flattery.

Josh sighed. "Kyla. She heard Jodie and I talking about it and threatened to tell you."

Hallie felt as though she'd been punched. Unwanted tears of humiliation and defeat filled her eyes. Kyla knew too?

"How many people know?"

"Just Kyla. And Jodie."

Hallie choked on a breath. She stood stiffly. "Well, you've done your duty. You are dismissed."

"It's not like that, Holly," Josh said quietly, but Hallie knew nothing except the hurt burning in her chest, a fire that was growing by the minute, threatening to consume her. She needed to get them out of her house before she succumbed to the pain.

"It is." She looked anywhere but at him. How could she get rid of them? Desperate times called for desperate measures. "And being the lazy person you are, I really wouldn't want to make you have to stay and put any effort into this confession or whatever it is any longer." She opened her front door, waving them out. "And please don't go away feeling good about yourselves. Honesty doesn't make up for playing with peoples' hearts. For manipulation and … whatever that unhelpful bromance thing is you two have got going on."

She knew they were looking at her as they left, but she couldn't meet their eyes. She heard their awkward goodbyes and final apology and shut the door behind them. Tried to breathe. Tried to hold back the sobs until Brandon's pickup turned the corner down the street. Then she collapsed to the floor and cried like she had never cried before. Everything hurt. Her heart felt like it had been torn in two. She could handle this from Brandon, but Josh …?

She didn't know how long she lay there before another knock came at her door. She pretended she wasn't there. But then Jodie's voice called through.

"Hallie? I'm coming in."

Jodie found her still on the floor and put her arms around her. "Shh, Hallie, shh, it's going to be okay. I'm here. I came as soon as I could."

Jodie helped her into the living room, sat her on the couch then hugged her tight.

"Oh Hallie." She could hear the tears in Jodie's voice. "They said you were just angry, but I knew better."

"They thought I was okay?" Her voice came out rough, her throat sore from crying. She blinked back more tears. "Do they think I'm inhuman or something?"

"Not inhuman, but maybe superhuman. You do come across that way sometimes, Holly."

Hallie shook her head, holding out her hands. "What's wrong with me, Jodie? Why am I such an easy target?"

Jodie sighed. "That's the problem, Holly. You're not an easy target and that's what made you a challenge for them. You seem so together, I don't think it ever occurred to Brandon how much this could hurt you."

"Do I really seem that hard?" Hallie's voice broke. "Am I really so devoid of feeling?"

Jodie looked troubled.

Hallie's voice trembled. "Please, Jodie. I know you don't want to hurt me, but I need to know. I know I can trust you to be honest."

Jodie took a deep breath and spoke gently. "I think you need to wear your heart on your sleeve a bit more, Holly. You can be intimidating sometimes with your intelligence, your control … this whole dignified lady thing you've got happening. It's easy to forget you're still young. Forget you're one of us."

Hallie stood on shaky legs, went to the kitchen to get a glass of water. Slowly she drank it before looking back at Jodie.

"But what if I'd let down my walls with Brandon? He wouldn't have respected anything I said. Is it any wonder I'm the way I am?"

Jodie's expression was filled with sympathy.

"And Josh." Hallie sniffled and wiped her eyes. "I just never thought … well, he's changed."

"He has. But things aren't always as they seem." There was something different in Jodie's voice. Hallie searched Jodie's eyes, but she clearly wasn't going to say anything else.

"Tell me."

Jodie ran her hands down her jeans. Sighed. "Well, he doesn't like people knowing, but I'm tired of all the secrets. You're family and you should know. He had an accident the summer he finished high school. It's no excuse, but it might help you understand."

"What happened?"

Jodie ran a hand down her face. "We were visiting our grandparents in Australia. He was playing Australian football and they don't use helmets or anything. He got tackled. Hard. He had to go to the hospital. He ended up with a brain injury." She blinked and Hallie's breath caught in her throat.

"Wh … why didn't I know about this?"

Jodie shrugged. "Josh didn't want us to tell people."

"But I could have been praying." Hallie's heart broke at the thought of Josh injured.

"Plenty of people in Grandma and Grandpa's church knew and were praying."

But she wanted to have prayed. She should have been told. She should have—

She caught her own thoughts. She was being unreasonable.

"Anyway, it changed him," Jodie said. "He turned down his baseball scholarship and pulled out of seminary. He hasn't played since."

"But he loved baseball."

"He used to love reading, too. He doesn't read anymore."

Hallie gasped. It felt as if a baseball had hit her in the chest, stealing all her air.

"He stayed in Australia for a year. I think his humor, his teasing, his flirting, it's all to help him cope. It's a cover for what he's really feeling."

Hallie tried to understand. "Why didn't he tell me?"

Jodie gave her a gentle look. "He doesn't tell anyone. You should understand how hard it can be to trust people with your weaknesses, your hurts."

Her words hit home. Hallie's lip trembled. "Does Brandon know?"

"Yeah, but not many others. Brandon arrived at the same time as Josh came home and they clicked. Brandon couldn't care less about baseball, and they both enjoyed video games and doing more practical things like doing up cars. Brandon took Josh to the gym, helped him with strength training to build muscle."

Well, he'd certainly done that. She tried to put the image of Josh's toned muscles from her mind. She didn't know what to think or feel. Maybe Josh really was someone completely different. But he still seemed intelligent.

"Did his accident affect his memory?" She held her breath,

waiting for Jodie's answer. For some reason it was important he remembered their childhood. That he still had that old connection, that memory of what she'd been through. Of what he'd helped her through.

"No. Everything else is normal."

Relief filled her. Followed by regret. She'd said awful things to both Josh and Brandon. She'd been ungracious about their apology. Yet she was hurt and frustrated that Josh didn't open up with her about his accident. She was a hypocrite. Josh and Brandon had made themselves vulnerable, confessed and apologized, and she'd thrown it back in their faces. She was just as human and sinful as they were. She needed to let them know they were forgiven.

But that didn't mean she'd be stupid enough to fall into a trap like that again. Ever.

CHAPTER FIFTEEN

Hallie waited for a chance to see Josh and Brandon, hoping to catch them together. The first time she saw them without other people around was on Sunday. They were leaning against Brandon's car in the church parking lot, observing the goings-on and no doubt gaining ammunition for their cynical conversations. However, this Sunday they didn't seem to be watching. They looked to be having a serious discussion. They stopped talking as soon as Hallie approached, both becoming obviously tense.

"I came to apologize." She spoke quickly, to put them at ease. "I said some things the other day that I regret."

"Regret? Because they weren't true, or because they might be hurtful?"

Hallie couldn't face Josh's direct blue eyes. Yep. Still intelligent. Too much so. She ignored his question. "I was ungracious. But I forgive you and hope you will forgive me for the things I said."

She rushed away, unable to handle anything else they might say.

She'd kidded herself that she was strong and in control.

Brandon hadn't been the only one who was acting. But instead of impressing people or drawing them to God, it repelled them. Made them feel inferior.

Take my fear, Lord Jesus, and help me always be real. Never let my heart deceive me again.

For a long time, she had refused to accept and feel her emotions. Self-control and goodness had been her protection, performed in her own strength. But it had shut out other fruit of the Spirit she so desperately craved. Like love. And joy.

Oh Lord, give me the fruit of your Spirit. Fill me. Overflow me. Teach me how to live and love.

Was that a knock at the door? Hallie looked up from her lesson preparation.

The knock came again. Stronger this time. Her head pounded. Josh and Brandon's visit and admission had shaken her in ways that went soul-deep. She'd almost prefer to face Malcolm than go through something like that again.

She came to the door. Josh stood there. He held out something wrapped in his jacket.

She opened the door and reached for it. "What's this?"

When he didn't answer, she took it from him and cautiously removed some of the jacket. There sat a tiny ginger kitten.

Hallie raised her eyes to his, searching.

"It was abandoned at work," Josh said. "It was curled up in the cool room, freezing its little … fur off. I thought you might like it."

Hallie laughed. Then she sobered. "I can't have it."

His eyes questioned her.

"The Junk Man—all his birds."

He nodded in understanding, then smiled. "Tell you what. How about I keep it at my place. I mean, it's yours and you have to visit it and give it attention and everything, but it can live with me."

Hallie's heart did a funny leap. Josh had found this kitten and thought of her.

"Do you want to come in?"

"Sure." He followed her to the living room and sat down. She settled herself across from him, the kitten in her lap. It snuggled into the crook of her arm and she smiled.

"So what do you think?" he asked. "Do you want me to keep it for you?"

She nodded. She wanted the kitten more than she knew how to tell him. When she looked up from the kitten again, he was studying her. Should she tell him Jodie had told her about his condition? No, but it was time she revealed a bit about herself.

"Do you know why I came here?"

Josh's eyes widened, then he frowned. "You don't have to tell me, Holly."

She ignored him. It would be a relief to tell him. "I came here because there was this guy back in Missouri ..." She blinked back tears. Why was it so hard? She felt so stupid. So naïve. "We had an internet relationship, and when we met in person I discovered he wasn't who I thought he was. I couldn't be with someone who lied to me, but he wouldn't leave me alone or believe that I wasn't interested. It unsettled me." That was an understatement. "So I came here to avoid him."

Josh's brow pleated. "If he wouldn't accept your relationship was over, that was his problem. Having an admirer is nothing to be ashamed of."

No, but believing he loved her was. And believing his lies because she was desperate to be loved? That was. Not that she was going to tell Josh that.

She didn't realize her hands were shaking until Josh came over, put the kitten on the floor and pulled her into a hug. He spoke into her hair.

"Hey, it's okay. You didn't do anything wrong. Maybe this gave you the push you needed to end up exactly where God wants you."

His deep voice rumbled in her ear. His chest was as firm as she'd known it would be. Everything in her told her she should pull back. He was comforting her as a friend, but she was feeling so much more. Her senses were going crazy. It scared her.

She jumped up, flustered, her face burning. She couldn't think. She knew Josh's hug didn't mean anything. She'd seen him give Rachel and Sarah hugs like that, too.

"Hey, Hallie."

She managed to stop and look at him.

"I wasn't messing with you. But you looked so sad."

She nodded. "I know. Thank you."

He searched her eyes then stood. "Well, I'll get this kitten home. Make sure you come and visit."

She nodded, and he tucked the kitten back into his jacket then walked out her front door. He bounced down her steps, turned back and smiled and waved when he saw her watching. She shut the door.

God, help me. What am I supposed to do about Josh?

HALLIE WAS desperate to see her new kitten. And Josh. His hug had brought back so many memories. And the fact that he'd brought her a kitten … But she hadn't wanted to appear too eager, so she'd held off visiting for a few days. Besides, it still wasn't wise to walk around town on her own. Sheriff Thompson said all had been quiet with Malcolm. They believed he would lie low for a while.

Thankfully her walk to the Ladans' house was uneventful. Aunty Lil opened the door with a beaming smile and invited her in. Josh and Brandon looked up as she came into the living room. They were sitting on the carpet, playing with the kitten.

Brandon quickly looked away, but Josh grinned at her, his eyes warm with welcome.

"Thought I might have to put this cat in the orphanage when you didn't turn up the last few days," he said, teasing it with a piece of string. "I thought it might not have been adopted after all."

The kitten pounced on the string. Hallie glanced at Brandon. What was he thinking? Had he and Josh been talking about her? Had they laughed at her, mimicked her?

Stop it. She had to believe they meant their apology.

"So are you her mother, or what?" Josh asked, and Hallie found herself caught up in his sparkling eyes.

She laughed softly. "Of course. Can't you see the likeness?"

Josh pretended to consider. "Well, I guess I can. You both have ginger hair and green eyes. Well, yours are blue but just as pretty. You're not covered in fur, but I'm sure you're just as cuddly."

Everyone knew Josh flirted all the time and his flattery was little more than waffle. Hallie was determined not to respond in case he thought she didn't realize that, but her cheeks flamed anyway.

Josh chuckled at her reaction. "Am I embarrassing you?"

"Not really."

He grinned. "So you're just hot."

"Sometimes the fear of blushing makes you blush." Hallie avoided his eyes. "And the more aware you are of your blush, the brighter it gets."

Josh considered her for a moment, then leaned back casually on his hands. "What's wrong with blushing? Is it so terrible for people to know what you're thinking or feeling?"

She was aware of the way Brandon's hand holding the string in front of the kitten stilled. Her mind went blank. Flustered, she bent to pick up the kitten and cuddle it close. The silence was long and awkward until Hallie regathered her thoughts.

"It's easier and sometimes safer not to open yourself up to people," she said quietly as she set the kitten back down. She took a deep breath and forced a smile. "Well, I've seen my cat's okay, so I'd better go. Catch you later."

"Hey," Josh called after her.

She turned back.

"Did you want to know its gender?"

Hallie blushed again. "Um, okay. Yes."

"It's a girl," he said. "Congratulations."

She couldn't help laughing as she walked out the door.

———

"WELL." Josh let out a big sigh.

Brandon shook the string in front of the kitten again. "That wasn't so bad?"

Josh shrugged. "I didn't mean to embarrass her."

Brandon picked the kitten up and settled it in his lap. "She's finally showing she's human. That's good. She's so reserved most of the time that it's impossible to know what she's thinking or feeling."

Josh nodded. He knew what Brandon meant. It wasn't that she lacked expression—it was that her expression was always the same. Always pleasant, always thoughtful, always mature and godly.

Apart from that time they'd shocked and hurt her with their confession.

"I guess that's the fruit of the Spirit," he said.

Brandon shook his head. "Nah, I don't think so. No one's that good."

"Not even with the Holy Spirit?"

"Even with God we still have emotions. We still struggle and go through pain."

Josh frowned thoughtfully. "So you think she's hiding her emotions?"

"Or denying them."

Maybe Brandon was right. Even as a little girl, Hallie had seemed controlled and together. He never heard her parents need to reprimand her for anything. She was nice. Too nice. He and Brandon were the only ones he had ever heard her say anything negative about.

Lazy, she had called him. How long had she thought that and never expressed it? How many other thoughts were lying beneath the surface of her pleasant exterior?

Josh had a sudden urge to know the real Hallie. The Hallie who knew and felt pain. The Hallie who made the occasional mistake or had a negative thought. He wanted her to let him hug her, comfort her like she'd let him do when they were children. Not like a few days ago when she'd jumped up, withdrawn into herself again.

Sure, she'd told him why she'd left Springfield, but he sensed it wasn't the full story. She was still holding back. What would it take to get her to open up and trust him fully?

Josh was on a new mission. He'd had enough of hoping Hallie would come to visit her kitten so he could talk with her. Jodie admitted she'd told Hallie about his condition, and yet she'd never mentioned it to him. Never asked him about it.

He stood at Hallie's door and knocked.

Hallie opened her door slightly and peeked through. When she saw it was him, she opened it fully with her usual pleasant smile. "Josh. What can I do for you?"

He narrowed his eyes. "You can buy me a new toothbrush, that's what."

"Why?" Her question was cautious, though she looked amused.

"Because your cat's been using mine." He tried to scowl but knew he was failing.

"Has she?" Hallie gave a little giggle then tried to cover up her moment of impulsive expression.

"Yes, and I think you owe me."

Hallie shook her head. "That depends. Where was the toothbrush?"

Josh pushed past her and into the house. "In the bathroom, of course."

"In the toothbrush holder, or lying recklessly by the side of the sink where any toothpaste hungry cat would be tempted?"

Josh sat down and threw his feet up on the coffee table. Hallie cautiously sat opposite him.

"I don't think that's the point."

"I think it is."

Josh studied her. She was still smiling pleasantly, and exasperation filled him. She was impossible. What would it take to go back to that friendship they'd had as children? Why couldn't she stop being so nice and pleasant and show him her heart again?

Frustration fueled his next words. "Well, next time I catch it with my toothbrush, it might just end up like your last cat."

Hallie let out a gasp. She stared at him as she processed his words. He wished he could snatch them back.

Her blue eyes narrowed, turning cold. "I should've known you can't help treading on anything that's precious to others." Disgust seeped from every syllable. "I'll get permission from the landlord to have my kitten here, and I'll collect her as soon as I can."

"Holly—" Regret squeezed his heart. What had he done?

"I'd prefer to have her here, battling the Junk Man, than to have you thinking you're doing me any kind of favor. You clearly have no respect for her and no respect for me. Please go."

His mind raced. How could he fix this? Before he could think what to say, she stood, marched over to him, and with one swift move shoved his feet off the coffee table.

"And if you had any manners, you'd consider my furniture and notice your feet are on my children's lesson material."

Slowly, Josh stood, seeing the fire in her eyes and wondering what had just taken place. He'd finally received a reaction just as he wanted, hadn't he? She'd lost her pleasant exterior. But she despised him right now and he wasn't sure he could take it.

"Holly, I …"

But she turned away, stalked past him to open the front door. He was tempted to make a teasing comment, lighten the mood somehow, but kept his mouth shut. It was only as he walked past her and tried to catch her eyes that he noticed they were sparkling with tears. He'd caused many girls to cry in his lifetime, but never felt any remorse over it, never felt this tight feeling in his chest.

This was different and he didn't like it.

CHAPTER SIXTEEN

Hallie awoke the next morning with a pain unlike she'd ever had before. She'd felt pain in her jaw on and off for a few days but had assumed it was stress-related. This morning, her mouth screamed at her from every angle, and a sharp, intense pain shot through her back molar. She wouldn't be able to work today, let alone walk to a dentist. She couldn't stand the thought of trying to talk on the phone, and so, finally, she made her way next door—something only a pain like she was experiencing could drive her to do.

The Junk Man saw her and waded his way through sheets of metal to reach her. "Are you okay?"

"My jaw hurts," she whispered, wishing she could stop the flow of tears.

The Junk Man's clear, intelligent eyes studied her. "Did you fall? Did anything happen?"

Hallie shook her head miserably. "I think it might be a toothache."

The Junk Man's eyes widened. "You've never had one before?"

Again Hallie shook her head.

"They can hurt like blazes. I had one once that was so bad that I took a pair of pliers and pulled it myself." His mouth turned up at Hallie's horrified look. "Don't worry. It's not something I would recommend."

To Hallie's relief, the Junk Man arranged an emergency appointment for her, and called Aunty Lil to drive her to the dentist.

Mac's fatherly care warmed her heart, and she pleaded with God to reveal himself to the Junk Man so he would spend eternity in heaven.

Forty minutes later, Hallie left the dentist minus one tooth. Aunty Lil took her home.

"You're coming to my house," she said. "There's no way I'm leaving you alone after what you've been through today. You need looking after."

Hallie didn't have the energy to argue, even though she would have preferred to be in her own little cottage where no one could witness her pain and trauma. She felt weak and didn't know if she could control her tears. What must the Ladans think of her, having to ask the Junk Man for help just because of a toothache?

Stiffly, she held herself up on their sofa, longing to lie down in her own bed. She could still taste blood and her stomach felt off. Josh wandered in with her kitten under his arm and grinned at her, igniting a feeling of dread.

"Heard you lost some weight today," he said. "I think you looked better before, though."

Hallie took a moment to realize he was talking about her tooth. The fuzziness in her head made it hard to think. Must be the painkillers the dentist had given her. She wished Josh would go away and leave her alone. He was the last person she wanted to see today. But he seemed set to stay. He settled himself into a beanbag and leaned back, watching her.

"I'd give you the kitten for comfort, but who knows what crazy thing you'll do while you're high on painkillers."

High was the wrong word for what she felt right now. She wished she had the energy and courage to tell him to go away. However, she could feel blood filling her mouth again, and quickly wiped some from her lip. Josh merely smiled at the sight.

"I'm sorry you needed a tooth pulled, but I'm glad you're here. I started to think you were going to avoid me for the rest of your life and I'd never get a chance to—"

"Stop it," she snapped. He could be so insensitive, so immature but she didn't have to take it. Standing on legs that weren't altogether steady, she made her way up the stairs to Esther's room to lie down. She would rather be in any room other than the room Josh was in.

What's happening to me, Lord? I don't like the way I am. I'm so ill-tempered and moody.

HALLIE WOKE FEELING DISORIENTED. It took a few moments to work out why her mouth ached and why she was in Esther's room. Then she tasted dried blood. With a start, she realized she wasn't alone. Josh was sitting on the edge of the bed, looking at her.

"Want a drink?"

Immediately, she tried to cover her mouth and felt the dried blood around her lips. "No thanks. I'll get it."

He put out a hand to stop her getting up. "Why can't you just accept my offer? I'm trying to apologize."

Hallie lay back, still tired. "Well, don't. And don't try to make yourself feel better by doing something for me."

Josh seemed to swallow hard as he frowned. "I know that's

the painkillers talking, so I'm still going to apologize." He met her eyes. "I'm truly sorry for what I said about your kitten, Hallie. I said it without thinking, and it was horrible and cruel and I didn't mean it. If there was any way I could take back what I said and make up for it, believe me, I would." His eyes were sad. "I was so angry with how your father treated you, how he hurt you, but I'm no better. You deserve to be treated so much better. You deserve more respect. More love. More ... everything. I'm so sorry."

He stood and left. Hallie watched him go, feeling dazed and confused. She didn't feel up to this. She felt weak and tired and no longer in control. More than anything, she hated Josh to see her like this.

He returned moments later with a drink of water and two Tylenol, which he held out to her. With shaking hands, she took them.

"I figured you wouldn't want anything to eat." He squatted down beside the bed to her level. "But I told Mom I'd come and ask you if you want something."

Hallie shook her head. He was too close. His eyes too warm and caring. His lips too ... She looked away.

Josh's warm hand touched hers. "Is there anything you do want? I mean, I don't have to get it for you if you want someone else to."

Hallie shook her head again, putting down the glass she was struggling to hold. Then she had second thoughts. "Josh, I want to go home." To her embarrassment, tears filled her eyes.

He studied her for a moment, then nodded. "I'll get the car."

As Josh drove her the few blocks home, he chatted away in a friendly manner that had Hallie breathing a sigh of relief. She leaned her head against the car window, then lifted it again when the movement of the car jarred her sensitive jaw.

"I'm thinking about quitting my job at the supermarket," he said as they turned down Main Street.

Her head jerked up. He glanced across at her and grinned. "You probably think I'm quitting because I'm lazy, but the fact is, I need more of a challenge. I'm not sure what exactly, but I'll find out."

Hallie would have asked how he planned to do that had her mouth not hurt so much. Instead, she listened as he chatted on.

"I've thought about working with children like you do. I have to admit I've had fun with Maddie."

Hallie managed to talk, but her words were slurred. "It's not just about having fun, Josh. Working with children is hard. You have to understand concepts deeply and thoroughly to be able to explain them at a child's level."

Josh didn't respond, and the rest of the trip was ridden in silence. It wasn't until he dropped her at her door that he spoke.

"Holly, how do I prove to you that I'm not a child?"

Hallie shrugged as she climbed from the car. "Know what you want and stick with it. Don't stop doing something just because it's hard or not what you expected it to be."

With that, she gave a quick wave and headed inside. She'd had enough of the day and was ready for a good, long sleep.

JOSH KNEW it had indeed been Hallie's painkillers talking when he saw her at church four days later, looking so much brighter. In fact, she seemed almost happy as she chatted with the church teenagers during coffee break. He watched the way her eyes sparkled as she laughed at thirteen-year-old Max. The teenager was playing with his mobile phone, programming in strange ringtones. He finally settled on an oink and put it down to take a donut from the selection of refreshments.

Then Hallie's slender hand came out and smoothly swiped Max's phone. She slipped it into her back pocket. Josh watched in astonishment as she then moved to some other teens and began chatting.

"You should ring Max's phone," she said. "He's got the craziest ringtone."

The teens immediately pulled out their phones. Josh grinned. The schemer.

Max heard the oink and glanced around. He frowned, looking at where he'd left his phone. The oink came again. He looked at his friends, accusing each one of taking it.

No one would ever dream it was Hallie. Josh wouldn't have believed it if he hadn't seen it.

Hallie was laughing. Even joining Max in accusing different teenagers of taking it in a rather dramatic un-Holly-like way. No one even thought to accuse her.

Josh must have been grinning more than he realized, because Max suddenly caught his eye.

"You've got it, Josh. Give it back."

Hallie moved to Josh's side and the oink came again.

She poked a finger in his face. "He's right. You do have it. I heard it." Her blue eyes were sparkling. "Give it back, Josh."

She reached up to pat his top pocket. Then she looked as though she was going for his jeans. He backed away.

"Oh no you don't, Holly."

"What?" She batted exaggeratedly innocent eyelashes at him. When had they gotten so long?

He watched warily as she sidled up beside him. He felt her touch the back pocket of his jeans. She was transferring the phone.

"Hey." He spun around, grabbed her wrist and held it up for all to see. "I've found the culprit."

Laughing, Hallie, tried to wriggle away.

He leaned close to her face. "You sneaky little thing."

"What?" Her smile took away from the innocent look she was trying to portray.

"What? This." Josh shook her wrist, prying the oinking phone from her fingers. "Pretending to be all mature and dignified. The real you is coming out, Holly."

His words wiped the smile from her face. She pulled her wrist from his hand and moved quickly and quietly away. Regret squeezed his heart. What had he said? Should he go after her?

He would, except he was too unsettled. He handed the phone back to Max, glad none of the teenagers appeared to pick up on whatever was between him and Hallie. When he'd watched her laughing, having fun … and then when she'd looked at him like that, the feel of her patting his chest to search his top pocket, her skin beneath his fingers when he'd held her wrist … *Oh God.* He needed help. Supernatural help.

———

HALLIE CLEARED AWAY the smaller Sunday school tables to make room for bigger ones. The craft group was meeting here on Tuesday, so rearranging the room for Uncle Theo was a welcome escape.

She didn't know what to make of Josh. His apology the other day had touched her. The more she thought about what he'd said, replaying his words over in her mind, the more she realized he was the same Josh she'd known as a child. He still genuinely cared. His heart was still good.

"Need some help?"

It seemed she couldn't escape him. She looked up to see him in the doorway.

It would be rude to say no. "Thank you."

He came in and took the table from her, shooting her a cheerful smile. "No worries."

She stacked a pile of chairs, then prepared to carry them to the side of the room. To her surprise, Josh leaned across and pried her hands off them.

"I'll take them."

She took a step back, blinking. "It's okay. I can do it."

"I know, but it won't hurt me to help for a change."

Understanding came. "You don't have to do this, Josh."

He didn't respond but the sparkle didn't leave his eyes as he carried the chairs to the next room. Hallie watched him go. He made it look so easy to carry such a weight. She shook her head. She was acting like an infatuated teenage girl.

Lord, my feelings are in upheaval. I don't even know what I'm thinking or feeling anymore. Help me. Please.

CHAPTER SEVENTEEN

Hallie walked into the Ladans' home with Aunty Lil for lunch after church to find herself almost bowled over and swept up in a hug. She stiffened, and the person gave a joyful laugh and stepped back.

"Sorry to scare you, Hallie. It's me, Esther. Esther Ladan."

Hallie's heart leapt as recognition filled her. Esther beamed, her eyes sparkling with joy the way Hallie remembered them. Esther was several years older than her, but she'd always made time for her. Esther was one of the most joyful, caring people she'd ever met.

"You're home." Hallie grinned.

"Yes. My boyfriend invited me to join him and his family in Spokane for Thanksgiving, so I've come home this weekend instead."

Josh came up behind them. "It's not the same as being here for Thanksgiving, Esther. You know that."

Esther drew him into an affectionate hug. "I know, little brother, I know."

Josh ruffled Esther's hair and looked at her with an even

deeper tenderness than she'd seen between him and Jodie. "I suppose we can forgive you. At least you came."

Esther pushed back from him and straightened her hair. "You have no idea how much I've missed you, Josh."

He cleared his throat. "I think I do, 'cause I've missed you the same."

Hallie looked between them, and an unexpected lump came to her throat. What would it be like to let Josh Ladan close like that? To trust him like Esther clearly trusted him? To have that same special connection she'd seen between them?

Or something more? She wasn't his sister, after all.

She looked away, embarrassed by her desire to be hugged by him. To be held close against his chest, protected and treasured.

———

JOSH KNEW he shouldn't have tried lifting so many chairs at once. His arm was tingling, a familiar and dreaded feeling. The beginning of a migraine. But he'd so wanted to do it. And now he wanted to spend time with Esther, but he needed to lie down. Maybe a ten-minute power nap would do the trick.

He lay on his bed and shut his eyes. It only took a few minutes for Esther to find him. "You okay?" The mattress sank as she sat down.

He opened his eyes. "Migraine coming."

"What set this off?"

He shrugged. "I tried carrying a stack of about ten chairs at church. And moved a couple of heavy tables."

Esther's eyes were knowing. "Why would you do that?"

He didn't answer. Because he wanted to impress Hallie, that was why. He wanted to help her, to have her notice him.

"What's going on between you and Hallie?"

And there it was. His older sister had always known him too well. Known what he wasn't saying.

He shrugged. "Nothing. She doesn't trust me."

"Because you're not yourself around her. That's what Mom told me, anyway. Does she make you uncomfortable, or does she bring back too many memories?"

Josh shrugged again, then sighed and shut his eyes. "Everything was good, Esther. Life was good. I was coping. And then … I don't know. She came and stirred things up. I went back to feeling like … like my life isn't worth anything. You know the abundant life Jesus talks about? I don't think working in the supermarket is it."

Esther smiled. "It doesn't matter where you work, Josh. You know that. All that matters is that you know Jesus. That you walk with Him, listen for His voice, love Him."

Josh bit his lip. "That's just it. I haven't been listening for His voice. I've been listening to my own. I got so scared of getting migraines, of doing something that might reveal my disability, of ending up back in the hospital, that I stopped living. Then Holly came along. She's been through trauma too. But she steps out of her comfort zone and takes risks. She believes God will change people, and she believes God will use her. I want to be like that again. I want to dare to believe. Dare to dream God's dreams for me."

Esther gave him a tight hug that brought tears to his eyes. "I love you, Josh. You are courageous. I saw you in that hospital fighting for your life. You are so, so strong. God gave you back your life and I know you're going to live it. I can't wait to see where He takes you from here."

———

HALLIE WAS worried when Josh didn't join them for lunch. She heard Esther and Aunty Lil whispering together as they sat down.

Jodie leaned over to speak into Hallie's ear. "Josh has a migraine. He used to get them all the time."

That was news to her. She focused on enjoying lunch with the Ladans, but it didn't feel the same without Josh. She hoped he was okay.

Her kitten hung around the table and Aunty Lil laughed. "She wants to be fed. Josh usually gives her half his meat at every meal. That's one spoiled cat, Hallie."

Hallie's heart warmed at the image of Josh sharing his lunch with the kitten.

"Did he tell you he's named her Bandit?" Jodie asked.

Hallie shook her head.

"Because she steals toothbrushes or something."

Hallie laughed. That'd be right.

Lunch finished and Hallie stood to help with the dishes. Aunty Lil shooed her away.

"No, no, you go to the lake or something. Spend some time together."

Hallie didn't want to go to the lake. Not while Josh was upstairs with a migraine. The pull to be with him was strong. Still, she followed Esther and Jodie out to Esther's car.

They got in the car and Esther turned the heater on. The air was getting chillier by the day.

Esther kept up her cheerful chatter as she drove, and Hallie struggled to focus. Esther parked across from the lake, and they exited the car together and walked toward the water. Hallie inhaled the cool, sharp air, marveling at the beauty of the mountains beyond the north shore of the lake.

Green grass stretched out to the west. To the east, she could make out the entrance to the campground. Sailboats drifted across the choppy water under a cloudy sky.

And there stood Kyla. Hallie's heart sank as Kyla marched toward them, then stopped in front of Jodie.

"Did you tell her?"

"Yes."

Kyla looked at Hallie, eyebrows raised. Hallie gave a half-smile. "It's okay. They apologized and I forgave them."

"Forgiveness doesn't mean you have to remain connected with them. The Ladans aren't the kind of people you should be associating with. That's why I left the church."

The temperature dropped fifty degrees.

"Hey," Esther said, "I don't know what's going on here, but I don't think this is helpful."

No. It wasn't. Hallie straightened her shoulders and stared Kyla down. "Kyla, I know you're trying to help, but I think you've made a lot of assumptions. No, the Ladans aren't perfect, but neither am I. We're all learning, growing. God's grace restores our relationship with Him when we mess up. Ours should too."

Kyla narrowed her eyes, lifted her chin, and walked away without another word.

Hallie wanted to run after her. Defend Josh. Explain what a caring person he was deep down inside. How his heart was soft toward God, he'd just been hurt. Like she had. Yes, he could be insensitive, but so could she. Josh was once the best friend she'd ever had. She'd loved him. She still did.

She glanced over at Jodie who was talking quietly to Esther, explaining what had happened.

"Josh never meant Brandon to take it as a challenge," Jodie said. "He just wanted Brandon to get to know and respect Hallie the way he does."

Hallie's heart did a little leap. She hadn't known that. Josh had taken equal responsibility with Brandon. He hadn't tried to make excuses or tried to explain. He'd been humble. Vulnerable.

"Of course he didn't mean it that way," Esther said. She looked at Hallie. "He still loves you, you know. I can see it."

"And yet he's dating another girl every week." Oops, she hadn't meant to say that.

"He's scared of commitment," Esther said. "He thinks he can never get married because he'd have to depend so much on his wife. He thinks it's not fair."

Jodie's eyebrows shot up. "He said that?"

"It was one of the first things he said when he was in the hospital in Australia. When he could talk again. He didn't just lose his dream of being a preacher. He lost his dream of being a husband and father, too."

Jodie looked near to tears. "I didn't know that."

Hallie frowned. "Why would he have to depend on his wife?"

Esther glanced at Jodie, then back at Hallie. "You know about his accident, right?"

"Jodie told me."

Jodie bit her lip. "Just the barest details."

Hallie's heart sank. There was more?

Esther led them to a bench overlooking the lake, but Hallie wasn't interested in the view anymore. Her sole focus was on Esther.

"We nearly lost him, you know. He spent three days in a coma and then when he woke, we didn't know if he'd ever speak again." Her eyes swam. "He fought for his life in there, fought with everything he had. I honestly thought we'd never get him back. But after a week he started walking, started signing at us. And gradually his speech came back. I know he jokes about being an Aussie, but it's all a cover-up. He blamed his slower speech on being in Australia so long, but it was actually the brain trauma. He wouldn't let us show anyone the photos of him with one side of his face paralyzed, his head shaved with a tube draining the fluid from his brain ..."

Hallie tried to draw in a breath. Couldn't. Jodie had told her about Josh having a brain injury, but ...

"His migraines in that first year were horrendous. He has to take it easy to avoid them coming back. Brandon has stuck by him. He's been a blessing from God. Helped him get back on his feet. Whenever Josh starts to overdo it, Brandon reminds him to slow down, but he also encourages him to try new things."

Esther looked out across the lake to the mountains covered with their first fall of snow for the season. "I know it's awful for him, living with a traumatic brain injury and Alexia. That's the condition that stops him being able to read. That part of his brain died and didn't repair itself. God can perform miracles, of course, but so far …"

Hallie tried to process what she was hearing. She felt numb.

"It's a strange condition," Esther said. "He can write, but he can't read. He can't even read his own writing. He believes that disqualifies him from being a pastor. I saw his hope and dreams die in the hospital." Her lip trembled. "He's so brave. So brave."

Esther remained quiet for a moment, then looked at Hallie. "I can't even explain what he experienced. People were dying in the ICU. It was a confronting scene. Josh had so many machines attached to him."

Hallie found her chin quivering. She'd just accused Kyla of making assumptions. What a hypocrite she was. She had judged Josh without knowing the full story. She'd even told him he shouldn't avoid something because it was too hard. Hard? Josh knew hard more than anybody. And she'd called him lazy. Been irritated by the way he was so laid back.

But he wasn't being lazy. He was caring for his health. Avoiding migraines. Dealing with a permanent disability.

Devastation at how she'd judged him filled her. She held back a sob. It was true she hadn't understood, hadn't known all Josh had been through. But she should have been the type of friend he could trust enough to tell. Like Brandon. She'd accused Josh and Brandon of being untrustworthy, but she was the one who couldn't be trusted.

Oh God, I'm sorry. Please give me another chance to be his friend.

Or something more. No, she refused to hope or pray that way. She didn't deserve him.

. . .

THE DESPERATION TO see Josh overcame Hallie's fear. The moment they arrived home, she made her way up to his room. The door was slightly ajar, and the blinds were drawn. She crept in and took a moment to adjust to the darkness.

Josh lay on the bed, eyes closed, a wet cloth covering his forehead. His cheeks were bristled as though he hadn't shaved this morning. To conserve energy? His bristled look had grown on her. As had his manly features. She studied his strong jawline and realized she loved the man Josh even more than she'd loved the boy Josh. Affection for him flowed through her, like water released from a dam.

Was he asleep? She stepped over the backpack he'd dumped on the floor. Not because he was lazy, but because he'd been too unwell to put it away. She knew that now. Holding back a cry she tip-toed to his bedside. Knelt down beside him.

"Josh, it's Hallie. I had to see you." Tears squeezed out between her lashes. "Oh Josh, I've been so judgmental. I'm so, so sorry. I didn't know, but that's no excuse. You've tried and tried to reach out in friendship and I've kept turning you away. Holding you at arm's length."

Tears trickled down her cheeks. He was so pale. So still. Was he even breathing?

"Josh?" Panic welled up. She grabbed his hand. It was warm and full of life. His fingers closed over hers and a faint smile tilted his lips.

"I'm listening."

She breathed a sigh of relief. "Esther told me more about the accident. About your time in the hospital, your brain injury. About Alexia. Josh, I had no idea of the extent of it. You keep everything so close to your chest."

His hand tightened on hers and he tugged her closer, pressing her hand against his heart. "I try to."

Was he cracking a joke? He opened his eyes to look at her and winced before closing them again. She hated seeing him in pain like this. Hated that she'd had no idea what he'd been through and had judged him for his struggles.

She licked her dry lips. "Well, I just wanted to see you. To tell you. I'll let you rest now."

His Adam's apple bobbed. "Thank you."

For coming to see him or for leaving? She watched him a moment longer, wishing she had the courage to wrap her arms around him. To bury her face in his neck and take away all his pain. To comfort him the way he'd comforted her as a little girl.

She crept out of the room.

Oh God, how blind I've been.

CHAPTER EIGHTEEN

Hallie looked down at the letter in her hands. The landlord had decided she could have a kitten in the house.

She should be excited. But if Bandit was here, what would be her excuse to see Josh?

It was strange, this desperate longing to see him; this fear of seeing him. She hadn't spoken to him since Sunday afternoon. Two whole days.

She was being ridiculous. With a sigh, she picked up her phone and sent a brief text to let him know she would collect Bandit soon.

Madison looked up from her homework. "What's wrong?"

Hallie smiled. "I'm okay." She looked over Maddie's shoulder. "Good work. Do you want to read to me now?"

Maddie beamed as she jumped up to get her primer out of her school bag. Hallie felt a lump come to her throat. Josh would never be able to read stories to his children. But he could still tell stories. She imagined him sitting with a child in his lap, coming up with funny voices. The child giggling, snuggling into his arms.

She had to stop thinking about him. Focus on Maddie.

FIVE MINUTES LATER, Josh stood at her door with Bandit in his arms.

"Thought I'd bring her over. Save you the trip."

Her heart did a crazy flutter at the sight of him. "Thank you." She tried to think sensibly as she led him inside. "It's not because I don't trust you with her. I do." Her words bubbled out. "But it gets lonely here, and you did give her to me, and ..." She smiled. "We can't have her eating you out of house and toothbrushes, can we?"

Josh tilted his head and gave her an amused look. He appeared much better today. More color in his face. Eyes open so she could see their beautiful color.

No. Stop it. She couldn't think like this.

"And this," he said to the kitten as he stepped inside, "is your new home."

Madison bounced up and down, trying to see.

Josh closed the door firmly behind him then placed the now half-grown kitten in Hallie's arms. She immediately jumped down and rubbed against Josh's legs.

"Traitor," Hallie muttered.

Josh grinned. He squatted down to eye level with Maddie.

"Maddie, your job is to keep Bandit out of the toothpaste and away from Holly's toothbrush."

He turned to go, but Madison grabbed his hand. "Can't you stay with us? Hallie was going to read with me."

Josh smiled. "Well, sweetheart, as much as I'd love to stay and hear Holly read, I really do need to go."

Hallie blinked as an unexpected lump came to her throat. He needed children of his own. The way he spoke so tenderly to Maddie, the way he made her laugh, the way he made her little face light up with joy. He was good with kids. And that meant more to her than she understood.

Josh gave them both a wave and headed out into the cold.

HALLIE HAD JUST ARRIVED home with Madison the following afternoon when her phone rang. She smiled when she saw the name on the display. Josh.

"Holly, I have your kitten here and she's chewing up all my toothbrushes."

Hallie gasped. "I wonder how she got out." She moved to the front window. "Oh, she pushed out the screen. But how did she find her way to your house?"

Josh laughed. "She's a smart little kitty. But I value my toothbrushes, so if you don't mind …"

Hallie smiled. "Maddie's been restless, so we'll put on our coats and come for a walk." She paused. "But I don't understand why you would have more than one toothbrush."

Josh clicked his tongue. "Because every time Bandit chews one I have to give it to her for keeps and get another one."

Hallie laughed. She and Maddie could walk over, but was that wise? Yes. Malcolm had wanted to meet her on her own, not in the restaurant. He wouldn't approach her unless she was alone. Besides, the latest reports said Malcolm was in Texas, nowhere near her. They'd be fine to walk. She looked at Maddie. "Want to go over to the Ladans and collect Bandit?"

Maddie's eyes lit up. "And see Josh?"

"Most likely." Hallie smiled as she spoke into the phone. "Josh, we'll be there soon."

Twenty minutes later, they arrived at the Ladans.

Aunty Lil answered the door with a beaming smile.

"Come in, get warm."

Hallie stepped inside. "We're just going to get Bandit and head back home."

Aunty Lil grinned. "Good luck with that." She nodded her head toward the living room. Hallie peeked in. Josh sat rugged up on the sofa with Bandit curled in his arms.

"Didn't know he could look so cute, did you?" Aunty Lil asked and Hallie felt the warmth rush into her cheeks.

"Josh!" Maddie ran into the room. "Can you play with me?"

Josh sat up and grinned. "Play what? Not Barbies, please. If I did that, you'd have to be sworn to secrecy. Can't have my manly charade shattered."

Maddie looked puzzled. "What's a manly charade?"

Josh looked over at Hallie. "Ask Holly. She's the smart one."

Hallie screwed up her nose. "Me? I can think of someone else around here who's too smart for his own good."

Josh ignored her comment and held up Bandit. "I can't get anything done with this cat here. Way too distracting. Just like its owner."

Hallie felt the warmth filling her cheeks again. Something about seeing a grown man tenderly holding a kitten warmed her heart. And the fact that he was so good with Madison helped his cause.

She took Bandit from his hands and snuggled the kitten close, trying to settle her crazy emotions.

Josh gave her a teasing look. "More likely she'll be back tomorrow. I'm her favorite person in the world."

Favorite person in the world indeed. Like cat, like owner.

IT WAS INDEED the next day that Josh called to let Hallie know Bandit was sitting on his shoulder in the Ladan living room.

"She thinks she's a parrot," he said.

Hallie pictured Bandit sitting on his broad shoulder and smiled. "Maybe you should just keep her there for a few days. I can't keep coming to get her."

"Why not?"

"Because Madison's only just left, and I've got to prepare the kid's talk for church on Sunday." And while she felt safer, she still wasn't going to risk Malcolm finding her on her own.

There was silence for a few moments. "I guess I could bring her around for you."

Hallie laughed. "What, and get up from the sofa? I wouldn't want to put you through that."

Josh chuckled. "Is that sarcasm I hear, Holly? Is the mild-tempered, always nice Hallie Hollaway being sarcastic?"

Hallie couldn't help laughing. "Of course not."

"And is she now lying?"

"Why don't you ask her?" She hung up the phone before he could respond.

A few minutes later, a knock came at the door. Shaking her head, Hallie went to open it. Josh stood there with Bandit neatly tucked under his arm.

She laughed and reached out to stroke Bandit's soft forehead. "How do you do it, Bandit? No one else can get Josh up from that sofa."

Josh's eyes sparkled. "All play and no work and all that ... don't want to make Josh a boll doy."

Hallie spattered out a laugh, unsure if he'd deliberately mixed up his words. Then she blushed as Josh pretended to wipe non-existent saliva from his sleeve.

He leaned closer. "Are you going red?"

"If I am, it's only because you're being ridiculous." She reached for Bandit. "And I've got work to do."

His eyes caught hers as he handed the kitten over. "All work and no play ... not the best idea either, Holly."

She bit her lip. "Actually, I'm learning that we need balance in our lives."

He grinned. "That's why we make a great pair, you and I. We balance each other out."

What was he saying? He bounced down her steps then turned to wave. "See you tomorrow, Holly."

Hallie shut the door and lowered Bandit to the floor. "Don't you keep going over there and forcing me to deal with him," she told the kitten. "It's getting way too hard to deal with Josh Ladan."

CHAPTER NINETEEN

Josh stopped in at Hallie's on the way home from work. He had some groceries for Madison's mother. Jodie had told him she was struggling.

Hallie answered the door and blushed. It was kind of cute that she blushed every time she saw him. He pretended not to notice, but he thanked God for the migraine, and that Esther had explained more of his condition to Hallie. She'd changed toward him. Softened. Become vulnerable now she knew his vulnerability.

He handed over the bag of groceries. "These were nearing their use-by date at work. I thought Madison and her mom might be able to use them."

Hallie blinked. Then she reached for the bag, glanced inside. A small smile came to her lips.

"I don't think Barbie dolls pass their use-by date."

He grinned. "Well, I might have just added that because … because."

"I'm jealous."

He laughed. "I can get you one if you want, but I would've

thought you'd still have that one Mom got you for Christmas back when you were a kid."

A shadow passed over her eyes. "My father made me give it away. He said I couldn't take it on the mission field because we needed to be above reproach."

Heat filled Josh's chest. "What? Barbies aren't acceptable?"

Hallie shrugged, then brightened. "It doesn't matter. Nothing beats the gift of a cat. You've already outdone yourself."

He felt the silly smile filling his face. Because the way she was looking at him now, he knew he'd finally done something right.

"Oh, I almost forgot. Mom wants to know if you can join us for Thanksgiving?"

Hallie bit her lip. "Isn't Thanksgiving family time?"

That's right. He'd insisted she wasn't family back when she'd first arrived. It was true she wasn't legally family … but she was growing to feel like … something more.

"Brandon and his mom are coming too. The more the merrier." He cleared his throat. "We all want you there, Hallie."

Her eyes glistened but she was smiling. "I'll be there."

———

HALLIE MET Brandon's mother for the first time that Thursday, and the woman surprised her. Mariah Taylor wasn't the classy businesswoman Hallie expected. Ms. Taylor was loud, rough, and critical of every person in town. Her main target was the Junk Man. Uncle Theo managed to smoothly change the subject and keep the atmosphere cheerful and positive. Hallie envied him his easy ability to connect with those who weren't Christians. He had a gift.

Listening to Mariah Taylor, Hallie also understood why Brandon was the way he was. No one could live with such a woman without picking up some of her habits. She knew Psalm

1 said not to keep company with mockers, but how did you avoid them if they were your own family? And how could you share the love of Jesus with someone if you avoided them? Despite her obvious faults, Brandon clearly thought the world of his mother. He made sure she was comfortable, and brought her anything she asked for.

As Aunty Lil ushered everyone into the dining room, Hallie breathed a sigh of relief and inhaled the delicious aroma of roast turkey and pumpkin pie. When they were all seated, Brandon passed his mom a bottle of sparkling apple cider.

Her expression twisted in disdain. "Where's the real drink?"

Brandon shifted in his seat. "They don't drink alcohol, Mom."

She laughed and swore. "That's right. I forgot Theo's the priest."

"Pastor," Brandon corrected gently.

"That's right." She swore again, then covered her mouth. "They don't swear either, do they?"

Hallie tried not to stare at the woman across the table from her. She acted drunk even when she wasn't. Or was she?

"Brandon, be a dear and go and get me a real drink," she said.

Brandon glanced to Uncle Theo, who nodded and mouthed. "It's fine."

Brandon headed out the door.

Josh kept the mood festive, making up crazy jokes that beat his father's bad dad-jokes. They ate and laughed until they were full.

But Brandon hadn't returned. Had something happened? Hallie's heart constricted at the thought.

"Do you think he's okay?" she asked Jodie.

"I hope so. He reckons he's the best driver out there. I hope he's right."

Josh left the table, strode to the front window, and peeked outside. Soft snow had begun to fall, coating the ground. First snowfall of the season for the town. Though beautiful, it brought shivers down her spine. Snow could hinder even the best drivers if they weren't prepared.

Brandon wasn't answering his phone. Josh moved away from the window and made them all play a game Esther had taught him—a game she played with her class at school. Hallie knew he was keeping their minds off their concern.

After another thirty minutes, the tension was like a fog filling the room. When Brandon still didn't answer his phone, his mother grabbed her jacket. "I think I'll drop by home."

Josh followed behind, grabbing a heavy coat from the coat closet. "I'll come with you."

As they opened the door to leave, headlights appeared in the driveway. They all raced out. Brandon's mother gasped in shock and Hallie covered her mouth. The front of Brandon's car was a mess. The black trim dangled from a huge dent on the front driver's side.

Brandon got out and crossed his arms over his chest. "A stupid woman stopped in front of me so suddenly there was no way I could slow down in time."

Jodie shook her head at him. "Thought you said you could handle your speed."

"I can."

"So how do you explain not being able to stop in time?"

He shrugged. "Sometimes meteorites hit the earth. Sometimes a friendly dog bites. You can't live around the possibility. You can't live in fear of something that might never happen."

Jodie held her hands on her hips and glared at him. "To some extent you should. There's a whole lot more car accidents that happen than meteorites that hit the earth."

Brandon glared right back at her. "Not with me. This was a once in a lifetime happening."

Jodie let out a long breath and her shoulders relaxed. "I hope so, for the sake of you and other drivers," she said so quietly Hallie almost missed her words.

But Brandon heard loud and clear, because he whirled away from Jodie and stalked into the house, his eyes dark with fury. If Hallie didn't know better, she'd think Brandon hated Jodie at that moment.

CHAPTER TWENTY

The Monday after Thanksgiving, Josh met Brandon for lunch at Joe's Diner.

Brandon slouched in the booth in the farthest corner, twiddling a straw between his fingers.

"Everything okay?" Josh slid into the seat across from him. "Did you get your car sorted?"

"Yeah. Easy fix when you work in the auto industry."

So what was troubling him? He waited for Brandon to talk. He'd learned Brandon would only speak when he was ready.

Brandon met his eyes. "Mom went for some tests a few weeks ago after she'd collapsed again. She couldn't blame the hot weather this time. She's at the doctor's now, getting the results."

Josh's heart squeezed with compassion. Brandon's mom was all he had. His Gilbertson relatives had all disowned him, apart from his cousin Becky. From their conversations at the coffee cart, Josh had gotten the impression that Becky hadn't told her family she knew Brandon.

"I'll be praying, Brandon. Can I tell Holly so she can pray too?"

Brandon grunted. "Yeah, but I doubt she will."

Josh was surprised. "Why not?"

"Come on, Josh. She's just like Jodie—treating us like wayward children who need reprimanding."

Josh studied his friend closely. Then he touched his shoulder. "Hey, it's going to be okay, mate."

Brandon almost smiled at the Aussie term for their friendship. He shrugged. "I know. I'm just worried. I mean, what happens if … well, Mom doesn't believe. It scares me, you know. I hate the thought of God being judgmental. I'm depending on His love and mercy, you know?"

Josh nodded. He knew exactly what Brandon meant.

"He loves your mom, Brandon. Let's not stop praying. Let's depend on His grace and mercy."

Brandon drew in a deep breath and gave a half smile. "Yeah. Thanks mate."

After they ate, Brandon headed home, and Josh prayed for him before going out to his own car. As he turned on the ignition, he felt a prompting to follow his friend. He sensed he was needed. He'd ignored the voice of God for too long, but no more.

Lord, help me please.

He arrived at the house not far behind Brandon. At the same time, Ms. Taylor pulled in beside Brandon's truck. He should leave them be.

He changed his mind when Mariah stepped out of her car and he saw her face. She was pale, but it was the terror in her eyes that sent his heart racing and his stomach diving.

He approached her. "Mariah?"

"Josh, I'm a goner," she said in a hushed, broken voice.

Josh blinked, swallowed. *God, help us, please.* "Let's go inside."

Inside, Brandon helped her into a chair. "Mom?"

Mariah drew in a shuddery breath while Brandon threw a panicked look at Josh.

Mariah looked at her son. "I have cancer, Brandon. It's got me."

Brandon's face drained completely of blood. "What do you mean?"

"I'm dying, Brandon. It's all through me."

Brandon reached a shaking hand for his mother's and Josh knew that his friend's world had just fallen apart.

"Tell me about your God." Her voice was pleading. "You said he forgives, no matter what."

Brandon nodded. "That's right. All you have to do is ask."

"And then I'll go to heaven?"

"That's right."

"Show me what I have to do."

Brandon looked helplessly at Josh.

Josh pulled out a chair and waited for Brandon to sit. Then he took Mariah's hand. "All you have to do is believe. Believe in Jesus and ask him for forgiveness."

Brandon took his mother's other hand. "It's true, Mom. "That's what I did. I realized I needed him." Brandon's voice broke.

Josh studied Brandon. The pain in his expression was almost too much to take. Josh was in way over his head.

"Would you like me to call my parents and have them come and talk to you?"

She nodded. "Yes. Yes, that would be good."

Josh took out his phone, realizing for the first time that his hands were shaking.

"Dad?"

"Josh." Dad's voice was warm and familiar in a world that was rocking like a small sailboat in the center of a stormy lake. "What's wrong, son?"

"Mariah Taylor's had some bad news. Can you and Mom come over?"

He heard Dad's intake of breath. "I'll lock up here and be there in about ten."

"Thanks, Dad."

Josh put his phone on the table. What his father did for a living was profound. Connecting with people at the most important times in their lives. Birth. Marriage. And death. Connecting them with God, ministering to them when they most recognized their need.

And every day in between.

As Mom and Dad knelt beside Mariah Taylor, tears streaming down their faces while she gave her life to Jesus, Josh wondered if this was what God was calling him to do with his life. He'd never felt as though he'd been part of something more powerful, more profound, or more important.

CHAPTER TWENTY-ONE

Josh sat in the living room, praying. Mom, Dad, and Jodie were praying too. Mariah and Brandon were coming to see them. It was urgent, Mariah had said. Josh knew whatever she had to say wasn't good. He'd asked Hallie to pray as well, and he knew she would.

The knock on the door pounded in time with his heart. He opened the door and allowed Brandon to lead his mom inside. Mariah wobbled as she walked, supported by Brandon, into the living room. But there was a peace in her eyes Josh had never seen before.

"I needed to see you all together." She twisted a tissue around in her fingers. "I spoke to the specialist today and it's not good."

"She has less than six months," Brandon said in a low, resigned tone, looking at his shoes.

It was strange that his mother seemed more at peace than he was.

"Yes, but it's okay." She patted Brandon's hand. "And I'm going to make sure you're okay. That's why we're here."

Brandon looked up, his eyes challenging his mother. "Nothing can make this okay, Mom."

She hesitated, then looked around at everyone. "I need to ask something of you, but I need to tell you all something, too." She leaned forward and took Brandon's hand. "Everyone needs a family, Brandon. When I'm gone, I know you will have the Ladans." She met Josh's eyes and he nodded.

"I'll be here. Brandon's the brother I never had." He tried to meet Brandon's gaze, but he was looking down, biting his lip.

Mariah drew in a deep breath. "And I'm going to tell you all the truth about Brandon's father."

Shock registered on Brandon's face. His head jerked up and his voice shook. "You said you didn't know him. That he was a soldier who'd probably died in Afghanistan."

"I know." Mariah's chin quivered and her eyes filled. "It felt safer that way. But Brandon, your father is Luke McAffrey."

"Who?"

Josh chanced a glance at Mom and Dad. Dad had frozen. Mom looked confused.

"Who?" Brandon asked again.

Mariah cleared her throat. "The Junk Man. Brandon, the Junk Man is your father. But he doesn't know."

Brandon jumped up, fists clenched. "The Junk Man? That strange man the children ridicule—who *you* ridicule?"

Josh couldn't believe it either, but Mariah appeared completely serious.

"I know, and it's unforgivable, but I didn't want you to work it out. Or him …"

Brandon collapsed back into the sofa with a moan. He covered his face with his hands. Finally he met his mother's eyes.

"What? How? Mom, he's so … weird. I always imagined my father to be, well, normal."

Mariah smiled and there was a faraway look in her eyes. "He

was, once, Brandon. He has a degree in environmental studies. He used to work for the council as the environmental planning officer. He's a very clever man."

The confusion in Brandon's eyes was heartbreaking. "But how … how did you know him?"

His mother swallowed hard. "I met him when my cousin Wayne Gilbertson was the mayor."

"And what happened?"

"It was all very complicated. An awful time. The only good that came from it all was you."

Brandon stared at his mother as though he couldn't believe his ears. "Mom, I need to know what happened."

She looked away, then back to him. "It's not a pretty story." She drew in a deep breath. "Wayne needed to buy some land by the lake. Expensive land, including the rowing and sailing clubs, and the camping ground." Mariah rubbed her hands over her face. "Wayne was mayor at the time, and a developer was sniffing around. Wayne needed Luke on board to adjust the records so the land couldn't be bought for development."

"Luke? You mean the Junk Man?"

"Yes. As the environmental planning officer …" She swallowed. "I was dating Luke at the time, and I needed a job. Wayne made me a deal …"

Brandon's jaw clenched. "Go on."

"I'd convince Luke to adjust the records so the area would be classed as a flood zone. That would drop the land's value, and Wayne could buy it instead of a developer." Mariah's lip trembled. "But Luke was a good man. I couldn't convince him."

This time it was Dad who encouraged her to go on. "What happened?"

Mariah swiped at her tears and her hands shook. "I was so angry that Luke wouldn't do it for me. I told him he would if he loved me. He insisted he did love me, but he valued his integrity. So I came up with another plan. I got him to stay at my place the night before the meeting. I'd been prescribed Ambien to help me sleep. I put some in Luke's wine. And while he slept, I deleted the reports he'd put together for the zoning meeting. Wayne uploaded another file to the council network, one that supported rezoning the land."

"No!" Brandon shook his head. "No, stop it, Mom."

"Brandon …" She reached for his hand, but he brushed it off.

"How could you?" He stared at her as though he'd never seen her before. "God might have forgiven you now, but how am I supposed to …?" He let out a sob, a great, rasping sob that came up from somewhere deep inside.

Josh had never seen Brandon cry before. He found his own eyes were wet. He desperately wanted to comfort his friend but he didn't know how.

"I stood up for you, Mom. I believed you." Tears streamed down his cheeks. "I ridiculed my own father!"

"Brandon …" Everyone looked at Jodie who spoke for the first time. "She's still your mom. She still loves you."

Brandon shook his finger at her. "Don't you preach at me, Jodie-Lee Ladan. Don't you dare. You have no idea what this is like. You and all your trite sayings and Christian values. You have no idea what betrayal feels like."

Jodie's face crumpled and Josh wanted to go to her. Instead, he went to Brandon and rested his hand on his shoulder. "No mate, we don't understand, but Jesus does."

The eyes Brandon turned on Josh were filled with such fire that Josh reeled back.

Oh God, help him.

Brandon charged out the door, and his mother broke into helpless sobs. "I'm sorry. I'm so sorry."

Mom wrapped her arms around the distraught woman and to Josh's surprise, Jodie did too. When Mariah was able to talk again, Mom spoke gently.

"Can you tell us what happened … with Brandon? The Junk Man?"

Mariah nodded. "Luke slept through the meeting. Wayne used the fake reports, and Luke had nothing to prove they were fake. He knew I had something to do with it, but he couldn't prove it."

"So why is Luke now the trash collector, not the environmental planning officer?" Theo asked.

"Hal Perry found out and made a big fuss about Luke not doing his job properly. Said Wayne only gave Luke the job because they were friends."

"But why?" Lil asked.

"Hal was always jealous of Luke, even through grade school, and he wanted the planning job. He was just as qualified as Luke, maybe more qualified. Wayne had to give in. He gave Luke a job as a trash collector instead."

Josh thought of the man so faithfully cleaning the areas around the lake, so carefully tending the wounded birds. The man had grit. He was loyal. But he didn't understand it.

"Why did he stay?"

"He loves Trinity Lakes. He knows every mountain, every lake, every road in the area. The house he lives in was the house he grew up in. His family are all buried here. He belongs here."

Mom stepped in. "Mariah, we need to get you home. You need to rest."

Josh noticed her pale face, her shaking hands.

"No." She sat up straighter, determination in her voice. "I need to finish this. I need you to know. To tell Brandon when he's ready to hear."

Dad leaned forward. "Would you mind if I recorded you, Mariah?"

"Do what you like. The truth has been hidden way too long."

Dad took out his phone and Mariah looked straight at it.

"This is for you, Brandon. And for you, Luke. You deserve to know the truth." She looked back around at the group. "I couldn't stay with Luke when he lost his job. My Mom was a judgmental woman. If I were to marry Luke, I would have been cut off. And I knew Luke didn't trust me anymore." She shook her head. "The day I found out I was expecting Brandon, I knew I had to leave. I didn't tell anyone. I just left and went to live with my parents in Vancouver. And I didn't come back until my parents died. They left me enough money to buy my own home."

Mom frowned. "What brought you back to Trinity Lakes?"

Mariah shrugged. "I can't even tell you, to be honest. The lakes? The need for closure? Until all that happened, Trinity Lakes was the only place that felt like home. My grandmother was nice to me. So was Wayne. Wayne's wife, now ex-wife, is another story." Her eyes darkened and Josh almost expected her to spit at the very thought of Mrs. Gilbertson. He understood.

"Maybe I wanted to prove something to Susannah Gilbertson. Whatever it was, I knew Brandon was restless and ready for adventure. He loved the thought of having second cousins he'd never met. Then the auto apprenticeship came up. It seemed perfect."

She looked directly at Josh and her eyes were warm. "It was the right decision. You are the best friend he's ever had. And now he's going to need you more than ever."

Josh nodded. He was inadequate to even begin helping Brandon through his pain, but he would trust God. There was one more thing he needed to know.

"Why all the trash talk about the Junk Man?" He saw a smile tilt Dad's lips and realized what he'd said. "I mean, why get Brandon to hate him so much?"

Mariah's lip trembled. "Brandon is all I have. I didn't want him to find out the truth about what I did and hate me. I couldn't risk Luke telling him. I couldn't lose Brandon."

"But Luke doesn't know, does he?" It felt strange to call the Junk Man by his real name.

"No, but he's smart. It's possible he's already worked it out." Her head fell into her hands. "Oh, how will either of them ever forgive me?" She broke into helpless sobs and compassion rose up in Josh's heart. He only prayed Brandon would feel that same compassion. In time.

JOSH COULDN'T SLEEP. He had an overwhelming urge to see Hallie. He didn't understand it except to acknowledge that she'd become important to him. He trusted her. Valued her wisdom.

He dictated a text to his phone. *You awake?*

He sent it.

It took a few moments, but her answer came back. His heart lightened at the smiley emoji he saw as his phone read back her text. *I am now. Is everything okay? You need to talk?*

He stared at his phone then texted back. *Can I come over?*

He waited for her reply. It soon came.

Give me ten minutes to get dressed.

Why did that make his face heat? He tried not to picture her in her nightwear as he pulled a pair of jeans and a shirt out of his wardrobe.

Hallie opened the door as he came up the steps to her cottage. She rubbed her hands. She looked all warm and fuzzy, wrapped in a dressing gown.

"I'll get the heater going." She switched it on, then turned to look at him. "I'm going to have a hot chocolate. You want one?"

He started to say no but changed his mind. "I'd love one. But you sit down. I'll get them."

She smiled. "Thank you, but I know where everything is."

She had a point. He met her blue eyes and smiled. "Okay. But one day I'm going to know where everything is in your house, and I'll get the hot chocolate."

She swept a strand of hair from her flustered face. Her rich, red hair was back. Only the ends remained dark now.

She ducked into the kitchen. A few minutes later, she brought out two steaming cups. She sat across from him on the sofa. Her face held compassion as she looked at him, waiting for him to talk.

It took a while for him to get the words together and retell Mariah's story. He watched the different emotions flash across her face at each part, from grief to anger to disgust to pain to compassion.

"How could she have got Brandon to despise and ridicule his own father?"

"I know. I still can't get my head around it."

Hallie looked thoughtful. "I guess everyone Brandon has made fun of is somebody's son or daughter or mother or father."

She was right. Of course.

"What do we do from here?" Hallie took a sip of her hot chocolate. "How can I help?"

Josh smiled. "Do what you always do, sweet Holly. Pray and love."

She blushed bright red and tried to hide behind her hot chocolate. "I can do that," she said so quietly he almost missed it.

She was amazing, this woman. So full of compassion and wisdom and commitment to God. What would Trinity Lakes do without her? What would he do without her?

CHAPTER TWENTY-TWO

Hallie was surprised when Brandon turned up at her door the following evening.

"I need your help," he said, his deep voice emotionless.

She searched his gaze. The storm in his eyes was something she recognized as pain. It was then it hit her. He had the Junk Man's eyes. How had she not recognized that before?

She opened the door. "Come in."

Should she tell him she'd been praying for him? Something told her he wouldn't appreciate knowing right now.

"I know I shouldn't ask you for anything, not after the way I treated you …"

She waited until he met her gaze. "I'll do whatever I can for you Brandon. All you have to do is ask."

He shuffled his feet then wrung his hands together. "I need you to help me talk to my dad. Tell him the truth."

Her heart stuttered. "What? Why me?"

He blinked hard. "You're his friend."

Hallie gave a small smile. "Well, I've tried to be."

He looked away.

"When and how do you want to tell him?"

His head fell into his hands. "I don't know. I asked Mom what she expects me to do with this knowledge. She said she expects me to do whatever is right." He shook his head. "That's such a cop-out. She's left it to me because it's too hard for her."

Hallie tilted her head. "Or does she want you to be able to make the choice? Perhaps she doesn't know what's right, but she trusts you will."

Brandon moaned. "But I don't know. He probably won't even want to know me. I'm the result of what brought him down."

"Or brought him up," Hallie said softly. "I don't think Mac is a less happy or valuable person because of what happened. Now he has his birds ..."

Brandon shook his head in disbelief. "I can't believe I'm hearing this. You think my mom did him a favor?"

Hallie didn't answer.

Brandon sat up. "Wait. What did you call him?"

"Mac. He said it's what his real friends call him."

Brandon shook his head. "For McAffrey, I s'pose." He sighed, and he looked so defeated.

Lord, help him please. Restore his faith, his hope, his trust in you.

Brandon shook his head. "I honestly can't understand why my father stayed here with so many people judging him, treating him like a ... well, like the Junk Man."

"Perhaps he has different values to the ones you've been raised with."

His head jerked toward Hallie, his gaze piercing hers. "What are you saying?"

"Well, the Junk Man isn't trapped by the need to be popular or to uphold his reputation. He doesn't need to bring down those who threaten his position. He doesn't have to constantly be aware of what others value and look up to. He doesn't need to perform. He lives by what matters to him. He gives from the heart. He lives with passion and compassion. He truly lives.

Every single day." She swallowed hard. "Like I wish I'd learned to do before I wasted so much time trying to be perfect and judging others for not being what I thought they should be."

Brandon stared at her. Then he sat back, his eyes never leaving hers. "Josh was right. You are a genius, aren't you."

Hallie smiled. "No. It's taken me this long to realize the truth, to understand what it really means that Jesus loves me no matter what I've done, no matter who I think I am. All that counts is who Jesus says we are."

Brandon leaned his head against the back of the chair. "And who are we?"

Hallie felt her smile growing as joy filled her heart. "We are His beloved children. Forgiven. Treasured."

Brandon rubbed his forehead. Finally he leaned forward. "I need to learn who I really am," he said. "Not just biologically, but as God's child."

"I'll be praying for you," she said through trembling lips.

"Thank you. Will you come with me now to meet my father?"

"If you want me to."

"I do." He gave a firm nod and headed for the door.

HALLIE KNOCKED ON THE DOOR, Brandon by her side. She couldn't see inside the dark house, but a shadow came down the hall.

"Mac?"

His raspy voice filtered through the door. "Coming."

She felt Brandon stiffen beside her. He'd probably never heard his father's voice before.

Then the door opened and Brandon was facing his father. Mac studied him, questions in his eyes. Brandon seemed unable to speak.

Hallie stepped in. "Mac, this is Mariah Taylor's son. He'd like to talk to you."

The man visibly flinched, then appeared to pull himself together. "My living room has some injured birds in it right now," he said.

"We can talk in my living room if you like."

Mac looked between Hallie and Brandon. "Okay."

She led the way, glancing back every now and then to see Brandon staring at his father. The disgust and revulsion she feared might be there had gone. In its place was confusion and wonder.

Brandon sat down first. Collapsed might have been a better word for it. Hallie sat beside him, leaving the other sofa for Mac.

He studied her with questioning eyes, eyes like Brandon's. Waiting.

Brandon appeared to find strength from somewhere within. He leaned forward, his eyes on the man in front of him.

"It might come as a surprise to you, but my mom is dying. And she made some confessions."

Hallie thought Mac might look interested or react in some way, but his expression didn't change.

"She ruined your job. And she lied to me my whole life. She didn't tell me that … that you're my father. Luke McAffrey."

Mac didn't say a word, but Hallie saw the way he searched Brandon's eyes. Then Mac looked down at his work-worn hands, then to Brandon's. He almost smiled.

"Looks like you're a hard worker. That's good."

Brandon made a noise that could have been a laugh or a sob. "I tell you you're my father who's been missing for twenty-three years of my life and you step in just like that? Like you've always been here with your fatherly advice?"

Mac shrugged, then ran a hand down his beard, revealing a

small smile. "I thought I might scare you if I jumped up and fist-pumped the air."

Brandon blinked hard. Mac's eyes misted.

Hallie pushed Brandon's knee. "Get up. Give your dad a hug."

Brandon glared at her, but then he stood. And Hallie watched as the Junk Man stood, threw his arms around his son, and held him close. She didn't know if it was their sobbing laughter she was hearing or her own.

CHAPTER TWENTY-THREE

Hallie watched as Josh collected scraps of paper from the floor in the Sunday school room. She refused to let him stack chairs now she knew about his migraines. A boy came in to collect his craftwork then held it up in front of Josh.

"Look what I made, Josh."

Josh stopped to look at the mess of crepe paper and glue.

"Wow. Is that …?" He looked hopefully to Hallie. She raised an eyebrow, and grinned, refusing to help. Let him work it out.

"Is it …?" He studied the work closer then smiled at the boy. "How about you tell me about it?"

"It's baby Jesus. Look. That's the manger and a donkey."

"Yes. I see it now."

The child let out a giggle and danced away.

Josh stepped in front of Hallie. "Did you enjoy that?"

She blinked, trying to look innocent. "What?"

"Making me guess what that mess was? I could have gotten myself into big trouble."

She bit her lip to stop her smile.

"I knew it." He shook his head. "You like to see me squirm like a little boy."

She laughed. "I do not."

His hands went to his pockets, and he studied her with raised brows.

"What? I don't."

He shook his head. "You treat me like a child."

"Huh. It's not like I lick my finger and wipe dirt off your face or something."

He laughed. "I'd like to see you try."

Was he challenging her? She searched his eyes. What was she seeing there? And why couldn't she pull her gaze away? He smiled into her eyes as though he could read her every thought. Her heart rate went up a notch.

Someone cleared their throat in the doorway.

Brandon.

"Everything okay here?" He gave them his smug, amused look.

On impulse, Hallie licked her finger and turned back to Josh. "Just making sure young Josh's face is clean before he goes back for more refreshments." She wiped her wet finger down the smile crease beside his mouth.

And froze at the feel of his bristled skin beneath her finger.

His mouth dropped open. His gaze locked with hers.

Hallie's breath caught. Touching him this way felt way too intimate, too personal. Heat filled her face as he grabbed her finger, breaking the connection.

What had she done?

Brandon laughed uproariously. She backed away from Josh, then turned and ran.

She charged outside to the children's playground, unable to think of anything except that she needed to escape Josh, escape the tenderness she'd felt as she'd touched him, escape her intense awareness of his strong jaw. She fumbled with the child-safe gate and let it fall shut behind her. She'd never felt so embarrassed in her life.

"Holly," Josh called from somewhere behind her. She didn't stop. She powered forward past the children until she reached the fence at the other end of the children's playground. There was nowhere else to go. She heard the gate to the playground open and close. He'd followed her.

"Holly. Where do you think you're going?" His voice held laughter.

She froze, then with a deep breath, turned to face him.

He stopped a few inches away and shook his head. "I can't believe you did that."

She wished the fiery warmth would leave her face, that she could look him in the eye.

"Me neither."

"I have to know …" He took a step closer, his voice low so that the children milling around wouldn't hear. "Was the mature, motherly, Holly flirting with me?"

She swallowed. Was she? She didn't know. Couldn't think.

He chuckled low in his throat. "Because that's what it felt like to me."

She drew in a breath, forced herself to speak. "I didn't mean to embarrass you."

He laughed and it was a warm, friendly sound. "I'm not the one standing here with the beet-red face. Brandon might never let me live it down."

She managed to lift her eyes. He looked as amused as he was surprised. She was just as surprised at herself.

"What did she do?" a child asked, and for the first time Hallie noticed they were now surrounded by children.

"Are you playing tag?" a little girl asked. "Cause you're s'posed to run, Miss Holly."

Josh looked at her, eyebrows raised. "They call you Holly, too?"

"Miss Holly is easier than Miss Hollaway."

His face softened, then he turned to face the children. "You all know I'm too lazy to bother chasing her. She wins."

Then he turned and walked back out the gate. Hallie watched him go, trying to settle her heart and breathe again.

SHE COULDN'T SLEEP that night. How could she have done such a thing to Josh? Her face heated and butterflies danced in her stomach every time she thought of it. And why was someone clanging on the Junk … Luke McAffrey … Mac's door? A harsh woman's voice was screeching at him.

Hallie peered out into the night. And what she saw set her heart pounding. An unfamiliar car was parked a few houses down. It looked luxurious, a model she didn't recognize. It probably belonged to the woman screaming at Mac.

Hallie watched as Mac's door opened and the woman charged into his house. Hallie crossed her arms over her chest and hugged herself against the cold.

Lord, what do I do?

Everything in her wanted to go and check on her friend. Brandon's father. To make sure he was okay. But was that sensible? Wise? She closed her eyes. It was about time she listened to her heart and believed God would guide her through it. She'd given it to Him. If she matched it up with His word in Micah 6:8 where He said to do justly, love mercy, and walk humbly with Him, then she was going to walk over there humbly, in God's strength, and make sure Mac was okay.

Just in case, she shot Brandon a text to tell him what was happening.

It was colder outside than she'd expected. She pushed open Mac's gate and went to his door. It was still open. The horrible woman with the screechy voice had him bailed up against the wall.

"If you don't get your disgusting, filthy birds out of here, I will personally make sure the council gets you out. You are visual and noise pollution all in one package."

Mac's voice was calm as he answered her. "Is this because you've been hearing rumors about what your ex-husband did while he was mayor and what his cousin did to get me fired?"

The woman looked like she was about to slap him. Hallie raced in.

"Mac, you okay?"

Two pairs of eyes turned to her.

Mac almost smiled. "Hallie. Meet my friend, Susannah Gilbertson."

Mrs. Gilbertson, with her glamorous blonde hair, beautiful makeup, and stylish charcoal pants suit, turned back on Mac, shaking a finger in his face.

"Hear this well, Luke McAffrey. You and I will never be friends." She hissed the word as though it tasted like poison in her mouth. "You are the Junk Man. Someone this town can well do without. I will start a petition. Show you exactly what the people of this town think of you and your feral birds."

Mac shook his head. "You should know me better than that, Susannah. I don't care what people think."

She sneered. "You will when I show the petition to the council, and you're evicted."

"I can't be evicted from my own house."

"But you can be forced to clean up your yard. Forced to get rid of your birds. So either you and your birds get out, or I make sure you do. And if I hear anything going around town about my ex-husband rezoning the lakefront land so he could buy it …"

Mac chuckled, looking at Hallie. "I think that was a confession. What do you think?"

The woman screeched and charged at Mac. Her long fingernails scratched his cheek and neck and her diamond ring sliced into his chin. He grabbed the woman's hands and held her off. Hallie stared at the line of red seeping through Mac's beard.

She needed to get out her phone. Call the police.

A car roared into the driveway. Brandon. *Thank you, Lord!*

Brandon charged into the house at the same time as Mrs. Gilbertson raced out.

"She hurt him." Hallie's voice shook as she moved aside so Brandon could see his father.

Mac reached a hand to touch his beard, which was now colored red with blood that dripped to the floor. Brandon glanced around at the towels and rags on the floor. Most were in use, with birds tucked into them, the livelier ones flapping and squawking in alarm.

"You got any clean ones?" Brandon asked his father.

Mac nodded and pulled a tea towel out of the cupboard.

"Hold it against your cheek," Brandon said. "I'm taking you to the hospital. And you have to make a statement against that woman."

Mac didn't answer. He allowed Brandon to lead him out to his car and drive away. Slowly, Hallie shut the front door. She wasn't willing to lock it in case Mac hadn't remembered to take his keys. She'd just sit guard from her window until he came home again.

It was well after midnight before Brandon's car pulled back into the driveway next door. Hallie raced out to meet them and stopped short when a stranger got out of the passenger side of Brandon's car, a stranger with a neat line of stitches down his cheek.

"Mac?" She stared in disbelief.

He grinned. "They said they had to shave me to stitch me up properly."

Brandon grinned the exact same grin. Hallie looked between

the two of them, trying to take it in. She'd never seen the Junk Man's mouth or jawline before. Only his eyes. But there was no doubt Brandon Taylor was Luke McAffrey's son.

"I'm going to get him a haircut to match," Brandon said proudly, following Mac to the front door.

Mac turned back, his expression wry. "So he reckons. Might take a bit of convincing to get the hairdressers in this town to touch me."

Brandon's eyes narrowed. "I'll cite all kinds of discrimination laws if they don't."

Mac didn't smile, but his eyes did. And the pride she saw in his eyes as he looked at his son made Hallie want to cry.

"Well," she said. "It's been a long night. I'm going to get some sleep."

Mac looked at Brandon. "You should too. You've got work tomorrow."

Brandon rolled his eyes. "Yes, Dad."

And Hallie did rush out then. Straight home to her bed where she had a good cry then fell into a deep sleep.

BRANDON PICKED Hallie up to bring her home from the Browns' the following afternoon. He also collected Madison on the way, to save her mom a trip.

"Thank you for being a friend to the Junk Man," Brandon said. Hallie tried not to wince. She imagined it would take some time for Brandon to get used to the fact that Mac was his father. She'd hoped, after last night, that he'd call him Dad from now on.

"Do you think everything will be okay?"

Brandon glanced to Madison in the back seat, saw she was busy playing on her tablet, and looked out the windshield. Drops of rain were beginning to fall.

"Legally he's only supposed to have up to four birds in his

yard down that end of town. The council turned a blind eye before now." He shook his head. "I want to get this all out in the open. I want justice. But my father wants me to leave it alone." He sighed. "Maybe once Mom is gone ..." He shook his head and his voice cracked. "I don't even want to think that way."

Hallie reached over to briefly touch his arm. "You need to think of the future, Brandon. What about if your dad moved into your place?"

Brandon's jaw ticked. Hallie fell silent. Was he still angry with his mom?

The rain got heavier. Brandon put on his windshield wipers. Hallie watched as the drops splashed on the road in front of them. Her laundry would be well and truly wet out on her line.

She helped Madison from the car, then waved to Brandon. "Thanks Brandon. I'm praying for you."

He nodded and drove away.

"Let's see if we can save my laundry," Hallie said to Maddie and the two raced around the back of her house, then stopped short. The line was empty. But Josh Ladan was carrying a basket of laundry up her back steps onto the porch. He gave her a sheepish look.

"It was starting to rain." He handed her the basket. "I didn't fold them or anything."

Hallie beamed at him. "Thank you. You've saved me having to put them in the dryer."

He nodded then shuffled uncomfortably. "Well, I guess I'll head home."

Hallie looked out at the rain. "Did you walk?"

He nodded. "Didn't expect the rain."

"Why don't you stay? Maddie and I would enjoy your company. Wouldn't we Maddie?"

Maddie grinned. "Yes, Josh. Stay."

He took the laundry basket back from Hallie's arms. "Right

then. Let's have a folding party, shall we? Hallie can teach me how to fold laundry properly."

Maddie laughed. "You're so silly, Josh."

Hallie grinned as they came into her living room. "Yeah, Josh. You're so silly."

His eyebrows shot up. "Me? I'd be careful what you say, Holly. I'm not the one who licked my finger and—"

"Okay, okay." Heat shot through Hallie's face. Flustered, she turned away, tripped on a chair leg, and found herself falling. And caught and steadied by Josh's arms. He grinned into her face.

"Falling into my arms, Holly? Got something you want to tell me?"

She pushed off his chest, moving away as quickly as she could.

"Thank you?"

"No, no." He shook his head. "About your feelings for me? You know what it means when you fall for someone, don't you?"

She tried to pull her thoughts together. Her words. Finally she shook her head, avoiding his eyes.

"That's crazy logic. I fell over the chair leg, but I'm not in love with it."

Josh let out a delighted laugh. "Good one."

Hallie couldn't help laughing too. He only thought it was funny because it was as bad as his jokes. "You're a worry, Josh."

"No. You worry, but that doesn't make me a worry. It makes you a worrier."

CHAPTER TWENTY-FOUR

I t was less than two weeks until Christmas. Hallie looked out her window at the sound of Mac's gate creaking open. He looked so different now he'd had a shave and a haircut, although he wore a beanie that covered his head today. Light snow flurries fluttered down, thick enough to leave small patches of white on the ground. Everything seemed to have settled down. Mrs. Gilbertson hadn't made good on her threat to get Mac and his birds out of his house, but neither had Mac or Brandon told anyone else what had happened all those years ago. Hallie had to wonder how long that would last.

To her surprise, Mac knocked on her door. She opened it with a smile and invited him in. He came in and sat on her sofa, but he looked uncomfortable. He held a piece of paper in his hand, flipping the corner with his finger.

"I've been pushed into a bit of a corner."

Hallie lifted her brows and waited.

He cleared his throat. "Brandon insisted on buying me a new work vehicle. One that has room for cages in the back as well as trash." He gave a droll smile. "And it's more powerful, of course."

Hallie grinned. "Of course."

"He wouldn't take no for an answer. Already bought it. And, well, I don't need two vehicles. Brandon suggested you might make use of my old one." He held out the papers to her and she saw they were registration papers. "I know it's not pretty, but it goes well. It's been faithful to me for years and I'd like it to go to a good home."

Hallie stared at him. "But Mac …"

He waved a hand. "No. Brandon did it to me, so you have to suffer the same fate." His lips tilted. "Friends go through that kind of thing together. So no payment. Just this awkward feeling of okay, but how do I say thank you."

Hallie laughed and reached a hand to accept the papers. "Um, thank you?" she said softly.

He grinned. "It's not so hard really, is it? Just forces us to swallow a bit of pride we didn't know we had."

She shook her head. She'd been praying about the need for a vehicle, especially now the weather had turned so cold. Never had she dreamed she would end up with the Junk Man's pickup. But she was so grateful. More grateful than she could say.

HALLIE DROVE her new pickup around to the Ladan's. She couldn't keep the grin from her face. What would they say?

Jodie answered the door and stared at the pickup. "Is that? That's not …?"

Hallie couldn't help the giggle that escaped. "That's my new car. A gift from—"

"The Junk Man?"

"Yes. Mac. Brandon supplied him with a new work vehicle, so Mac supplied me with my very own vehicle."

Jodie shook her head. Hallie understood. She couldn't quite get her head around it either.

"Josh," she called. "Come and check out Hallie's new set of wheels."

Josh came to the door, followed by Aunty Lil. They both laughed when they heard the story.

"God provides in mysterious ways," Aunty Lil said as they came inside and sat together in the living room.

"Speaking of which ..." Josh looked at Hallie. "I'm hoping you're God's provision to get me out of an awkward situation."

Hallie bit her lip, wondering what was coming next. Josh looked to Aunty Lil.

"It was Mom's idea, so don't worry. And I think it's a good one."

"Okay ..."

"I've been invited to the Bible college Christmas dinner. I'm supposed to bring a date. Jodie doesn't want to come. Sarah heard about it and is hinting I should take her. And, well ... Mom says that because you're family ... I could take you instead."

But he didn't look exactly happy about it. What was she supposed to make of that?

Aunty Lil looked excited. "Tell her why you're invited, Josh."

Josh suddenly looked awkward. He rubbed his forehead. "Well, I've applied to go to Bible college next year."

"And been accepted," Aunty Lil said.

"Just to study part time," he said. "Two classes per semester instead of four, and they agreed to provide special accommodations. Haven't quite worked all those out yet, but I have some ideas of what would work, and so does Esther. I'll still work at Lakes Fresh Food, so I can pay my way."

Hallie blinked, her heart stuttering at the news. She opened her mouth. Closed it again.

Josh smiled at her unspoken questions. "I want to follow God's plan for my life. And when I saw what Dad did for Brandon's mom ... I realized my heart has never changed. I still want to be a pastor. God didn't change my calling when I got my brain injury. He just made me so I'm more aware of my need of Him."

Unexpected emotion clogged Hallie's throat.

"So will you go to the dinner with him?" Jodie looked pleased with the idea.

Josh looked at his sister, then to his mother. "Do you mind if I talk to Hallie alone for a minute?"

Jodie's face fell, but she followed Aunty Lil from the room.

Hallie was left alone looking at Josh. He fiddled with the band of his watch.

"Well, this is awkward." He chuckled.

Hallie's heart sank. She'd known he didn't really want to.

"I know Mom is always going on about you being family, but I want you to come with me as … as a real date. Not as a sister. Or an excuse to give Sarah." His eyes captured and held hers, questioning and hopeful. "If you want to."

She smiled. He was adorable looking at her all hopeful and shy like that. "I'd love to come."

"Really?" He beamed at her. Then he cleared his throat again, the vulnerability returning. "If you wouldn't mind, I might need help with reading the order of proceedings or menu on the night."

She smiled, tears stinging her eyes. He finally trusted her. "It would be my honor."

His eyes took on a playful gleam. "And in return I'll happily lick my finger and clean your face if you get any food on it."

She bit her lip. "Josh. Are you ever going to let me live that down?"

He grinned. "Not likely."

JODIE INSISTED on helping Hallie get ready for her date with Josh.

"It's just a date," she reminded Jodie. "It's not like I'm the first girl he's ever taken on a date."

Jodie gave a knowing smile as she pulled strands of Hallie's hair into a braid. "But I expect you'll be the last." She sprayed hair spray over Hallie's hair, then turned her around.

"Beautiful," she whispered.

Hallie looked down at her blue dress. Jodie had helped her find it. She had to admit it was stunning and it brought out her eyes. She felt beautiful tonight.

Jodie beamed. "Let's show Josh."

Hallie's stomach filled with nerves. What would Josh think of how she looked? Would he enjoy her company, or just use her to make a point to Sarah? She needed to guard her heart. But telling herself that wasn't working.

Josh's eyes lit up when he saw her. He held out his arm. "May I escort you to dinner?"

She gave a nervous laugh. "You may."

The sight of Josh Ladan in a suit and tie made it hard to breathe. She swallowed hard as he came to her side, placed her arm in his, and led her out to his car. It felt as though she were walking beside a stranger. But it was him. Tall. Strong. Masculine. He turned and met her eyes, letting out his familiar slow smile. She looked away, self-conscious, yet was aware of his gaze on her. She expected him to make a flirtatious comment, but he opened the car door for her without saying a word.

The Bible college's dining hall was decorated with twinkling Christmas lights and large round tables set for eight.

Josh leaned to whisper in her ear. "Can you find our place cards? I'll get a migraine looking at them all."

Her heart softened with compassion. "Of course." She led him around, searching for their cards until she finally found them.

"This is our place." No one else was at the table yet.

He pulled out her chair for her. She sat, wondering if he felt as awkward and out of place as she did, all dressed up. Blushing under his unusually serious gaze, she fiddled with her cutlery.

"Well." Josh grinned, as though breaking out of a dream. "Just you and me. This sets the scene for romance."

"It certainly does," Hallie chuckled, relieved to have the familiar, light-hearted Josh back. "As if you'd know anything about true romance. It's too hard work for you to want to explore."

"You'd be surprised."

Hallie laughed. "You plan to surprise me tonight?" Immediately she wished she could take back her words. She hadn't meant to flirt.

He grinned as though he knew what she was thinking. "Nah. I wouldn't know how to romance you. You're too … mature. Your humor died with your childhood. Now the fun-loving Holly of fifteen years ago might have been different."

"I see." Hallie smiled at him. "You've charmed all your previous dates with your superb sense of humor."

"Exactly. So tonight is going to be hard work without that as my secret weapon."

She couldn't help the laugh that burst out.

Moments later, more people arrived and she pulled herself together. An older couple joined the table. Hallie recognised them from church. The man sometimes took Uncle Theo's place preaching. She had appreciated his challenging sermons and his heart for God. She also enjoyed his Australian accent which was much like Aunty Lil's.

The man dipped his head to acknowledge Josh. "Joshua Ladan. Who's your friend?"

Josh smiled at Hallie, a tender, exclusive kind of smile that made her feel shy. And special. "This is Hallie. Her parents studied here fifteen years ago. Hallie, this is the college Director, Mr. Franklin."

The Director shook her hand. "Nice to meet you, Hallie.

Call me Peter." He turned back to Josh. "We're looking forward to having you next year. If you live up to the Ladan name …"

Josh shook his head. "I can only dream of being a man like my father. To be honest, I think one of the reasons I put Bible college off for so long was my fear of being a disappointment. With Dad lecturing here and so many people knowing him … it's a hard act to follow."

Peter smiled. "You'll do just fine, son. God has given you gifts of your own. As much as I admire your humility, I hope you'll allow God to show you exactly how important the ministry he has specifically for you will be."

Josh nodded, looking uncomfortable. "Yes, sir," he said.

Without thought, Hallie reached for his hand under the table and gave it a squeeze. Just for support. To her surprise, he didn't allow her to pull away. Instead, he threaded his fingers through hers. She looked up at him.

He winked and her heart warmed.

Uncle Theo came over to the table and shook Peter Franklin's hand. Then he leaned down and spoke quietly.

"You look convincing, Josh, but Hallie, you'd better pick up your act if you want Sarah to leave Josh alone."

Hallie's mouth dropped open as she darted a look at Josh. He was gazing at her with a soft expression on his face. Her heart gave a funny leap at the way he leaned in, a tender look in his eyes.

"Ignore him." His breath tickled her ear. "Dad doesn't know when to leave his bad jokes at home."

She smiled affectionately at him. "Like father, like son."

"Hey—" He pulled back, but his eyes were twinkling.

Peter leaned across to speak to Hallie. "So your parents studied here?"

Hallie nodded. "Yes. John and Jane Hollaway."

"Ah, yes, I remember now. Missionaries, aren't they?"

Hallie tensed, but relaxed when Josh's warm hand squeezed hers under the table.

"Yes, they are," he said on her behalf.

"We've got another former missionary here tonight." Peter gestured toward a round table at the far end of the room where two men sat conversing, one taller, one shorter. "The gentleman with brown hair, Dr. Dylan MacKay, used to be a missionary. He's just arrived from Australia, and will be guest lecturing at the seminary for us this semester."

Hallie studied the man. His aloof, somber demeanor was in stark contrast to the exuberant expressive nature of his friend, who seemed able to hold the attention of the entire table.

Hallie expelled a breath and glanced at Josh. The last thing she wanted to talk about was missionaries. No offense to Dr. MacKay.

Josh cleared his throat and smiled brightly. "I hear your daughter is soon to be married?"

It was the perfect diversion. Peter beamed with pride as he told them all about Lexi, who had met a local rancher and fallen head over heels in love. His wife added details to the story and Hallie found herself getting teary. It was so romantic.

This whole scene was romantic. Josh sitting with his arm around her, catching her eye every now and then, smiling softly, listening to the Franklins share about their daughter finding her soulmate.

Josh didn't need humor to charm her. He just needed to be there.

———

NEITHER SPOKE as Josh drove Hallie home. He was trying to sort through his crazy emotions. No other date had left him feeling this way. His heart felt exposed yet so full.

She'd looked like an angel with the tiny lights shining down on her. Her blue eyes shone and sparkled when she laughed. At times she'd looked confused and a vulnerable look passed over her face. He understood. This was new ground for both of them.

He pulled up in front of her house and turned in his seat to face her. "Well, that was quite an experience."

She smiled. "It was. But I thought you said tonight would be hard for you. It seemed to all come naturally. I guess all that practice has made you a pro."

She was teasing him. But did she know the truth? He blew on his hands and turned up the heater. "It was hard," he said. "In ways you wouldn't understand."

"Try me."

He smiled. "Someday. Not tonight." She was clearly wanting to keep the atmosphere light-hearted for now and he'd follow her lead.

She tilted her head, studying him. "Do you think Sarah is convinced now?"

He grinned. "From my end, yes. But you heard my dad … it would have been nice if you'd tried to be more convincing. It's not good for my ego to have a woman not returning my attentions."

"Josh Ladan, I think your ego is perfectly intact. It does not need my help."

"I dunno." He reached over and flicked a strand of her soft hair. "It certainly didn't help a few Sundays back when a woman licked her finger and wiped it down my face like I was some messy little kid."

"Josh …" Her face flamed.

He reached for her hand and traced the soft skin on her fingers. Her blue eyes widened. What would she do if he kissed her? She pulled her hand from his before he could make up his mind.

"I have to do the kid's talk in church tomorrow. I'd better get some sleep."

She opened the door and looked back at him, that vulnerable expression on her face again.

"Thank you for being my date, Holly," he said. "Really."

"You're welcome."

He watched as she turned and walked up the path to her front door. Tall, poised, and beautiful.

CHAPTER TWENTY-FIVE

Hallie hadn't felt uncomfortable at church before, but today she couldn't bring herself to look directly at Josh. Last night had been confusing. He was confusing. She didn't go in to help clear the Sunday School room. Josh and Brandon could manage without her.

Jodie cornered her outside. "Tell me all about it," she commanded, eyes shining. "Was he romantic?"

Hallie rolled her eyes. "He flirted like usual." Except that wasn't quite true.

Jodie stiffened and Hallie followed her gaze.

Josh and Brandon were heading their way.

Brandon nodded at them. "How's it going, girls?"

Jodie scowled. "I'm now nineteen years old, Brandon."

Brandon smirked. "My apologies. Ladies."

Jodie looked at Josh. "I was asking Hallie all the sickening details of your date, since you won't tell me anything. It seems she won't either. Is that because you're both trying to hide something? Like, let's say, a passionate goodnight kiss?"

Josh screwed up his nose. "We didn't go that far."

Hallie tried not to be offended by his reaction.

Brandon winked at Hallie. "You don't know what you missed."

If Josh was playing it cool, she would too. "I think I do, and I don't mind."

Brandon shook his head. "Holly, Holly, many girls consider Josh very desirable, and I've heard them say that when it comes to kissing, well …"

Hallie laughed but her face heated. "Josh would be a hopeless kisser. Who can kiss properly with their hands in their pockets and a silly grin on their face?"

Josh raised his eyebrows. "You reckon I kiss like that?"

Her mouth went dry. "Umm …"

He moved toward her, a dangerous glint in his eyes. "You know I'm going to have to prove you wrong now, don't you?"

She put her hands on his chest to hold him back, cheeks flaming. "Not with me."

He chuckled. "I'm not meaning to practice cheek pecks, Holly. It's inappropriate to kiss Jodie that way. I'd give her a heart attack."

"Me too." The way her heart was thumping now she didn't think she was exaggerating.

He pulled a disappointed face. "Then who am I supposed to practice on?"

"Josh Ladan, I've no doubt you've had plenty of practice." And that was the problem. She had never kissed anyone that way before. Ever.

Josh shrugged and grinned, leaning back on the wall behind him. "I think you're making assumptions again."

He was right. She was. Was she judging him unfairly?

He reached over and ran a finger down her cheek. "But I forgive you." Then he walked away, Brandon following close behind.

Hallie glanced over at Jodie. "Who is that man?"

Jodie shook her head. "I have no idea."

. . .

HALLIE DROVE HOME Monday evening with her shopping bags in the front seat of the pickup. She was surprised how many people waved to her, thinking she was the Junk Man. It seemed he did have friends around town. She turned the corner toward home and slammed on the brakes. There, parked in front of her house, was an unfamiliar car with Idaho plates. She drove slowly past her driveway. No one was in sight.

She let out a wry laugh. She had a phobia now. It could be anyone. Maybe someone was looking for Mac, or visiting a friend down the street.

Still, she couldn't bring herself to pull into her driveway. Instead, she headed to the Ladans. As she walked up to their front door, she hesitated. What was she doing? It was silly to avoid her own house just because of a car. Trinity Lakes was a tourist town, after all. Undecided, she lifted her hand to knock, then let it fall.

She turned back around to head home and bumped hard into someone. She couldn't stop the scream that escaped.

"Jumpy, aren't we?" Josh's voice laughed as his hands came to her shoulders, steadying her.

Shakily, Hallie laughed, too. He was too close. The strength of his hands on her shoulders … She took a step back. "You would be too, if you turned around and someone like you was standing there."

Josh pulled a face, but his eyes were twinkling with amusement. "That's nasty. Had a hard day?"

"Yeah, I guess I have." All because of a car.

Josh opened the door and held it, waiting for her to enter. Hallie took a last glance back over her shoulder onto the street.

Josh looked out onto the street too then looked back at her. "Everything okay?"

She forced herself to relax. "Yeah. I'm fine." She knew she

didn't sound convincing. Josh continued to study her. He followed her into the kitchen where she helped herself to a drink.

"So what happened?" Genuine care showed in his eyes.

How to answer without answering? She pulled her gaze from his and saw the photo on the fridge. Her and her parents. Why did it make her want to cry?

Josh followed her gaze, then shot her a thoughtful look. He pulled the photo off the fridge and studied it. "You were never allowed to be a child, were you?"

She couldn't look at him. When she didn't answer, he continued.

"I used to be amazed at how they treated you like an adult. But then, you always acted like one."

She managed to look at him. "I had to be an adult. They had an important ministry. I couldn't afford to be ..." What? A problem? "A child," she said.

"They didn't show you much love or affection." His eyes softened, taking away the sting of his words. "Is that why you shy away from affection? You've never experienced it?"

The tender, caring tone of his voice was too much. Her throat burned. The fact that this conversation was making her so uncomfortable proved the truth of his words.

She took the photo from his hands and focused on placing it neatly back on the fridge. "I don't shy away from affection." That came out more defensive than she'd intended. And they both knew it wasn't true. Hadn't she jumped out of the car the other night when she'd thought he might kiss her? Hadn't she both feared it and desired it at the same time? "I'm not scared," she said, determined to make herself believe it.

Josh flashed a grin and the atmosphere changed. His eyes took on their usual twinkle. He stepped closer.

"Is that right?"

Her breath caught. His eyes held hers.

"Because Jodie is still at work, which means we have the opportunity right now for you to prove you're not scared." He tilted his head to the side. "Or we could practice anything you might need practice at …"

He was back to his light-hearted, flirty self. And yet something in his eyes drew her, told her there was something deeper behind his teasing. She needed to get out of here. Get her feelings under control.

She backed away. "I'd better get home, actually."

He threw a hand to his heart. "Oh, and here I was thinking you might be getting the hang of romance. But no, the old Hallie is back in full force. Next you'll be licking your hand and patting down my hair like you're my mother."

She glanced at his hair. Thick and healthy. Sitting … perfectly. Definitely not a good idea to touch it. Or him. She glanced away.

"I'm thinking your hair looks a bit wild, though." He moved into her space. "And is that dirt I see on your face? Maybe I need to clean it off for you." He licked his finger.

She shoved him in the chest with both hands and spun away. Just to be safe she grabbed a used glass from the bench and splashed him with the few drops left in the bottom.

Josh's eyebrows shot up and he laughed. "And there I was feeling sorry for you, and thinking I should stop teasing you."

Hallie backed away, but he kept coming. The fridge against her back stopped her progress. He smiled. Slow and triumphant.

A sound shattered the silence. She screamed and grabbed her chest.

"Hey, it's just the doorbell." Josh shot her a look of concern before going to get the door.

Her nerves were so on edge.

Brandon came into the house and gave Hallie a quick smile. "How's it going, Holly?"

She tried to smile, willing her heart to slow down. "I'm good, but I better get going."

Brandon smirked. "Did I interrupt something?"

"Yes," Josh said.

"No," Holly said at the same time.

Brandon's smirk grew. "Right."

Blushing, Hallie waved and rushed out the door. What would have happened if Brandon hadn't turned up? And why was she disappointed he had?

THE CAR WAS STILL in front of her house. Hallie went to Mac's door first and knocked.

His door swung open, and it took her a moment to realize it was him. It was hard to get used to his clean-shaven look.

"Mac, do you know anything about the car parked out the front of my place?"

Mac shook his head. "No, but sometimes tourists park in weird places. An older couple walked past with their dog earlier. Set my geese off something crazy. Might be visitors finding somewhere to park so they can take a walk around town."

Hallie frowned. She hoped so, but she couldn't imagine anyone taking a stroll in this cold, biting wind.

"It making you nervous?" Mac asked.

Hallie drew in a deep breath. "I'm being silly. It's fine."

Mac's eyes narrowed as though he knew she wasn't telling him something. "Well, I'm not going anywhere. I'll be right next door if that helps you feel better."

Hallie smiled. "It does. Thank you."

Embarrassed by her own insecurities, she forced herself to go home. Her door was locked just the way she'd left it. Nothing seemed disturbed. She unpacked her groceries and kicked off her shoes, ready to relax for the evening, then looked around for Bandit.

"Bandit, where are you?" Normally Bandit was all over her when she first arrived home. She enjoyed the affection the kitten offered. Not that she was a kitten anymore. She'd grown fast. Like Josh had grown on her.

She'd bet Bandit had escaped again. If so, Josh would be here any minute to return her. Yes, the front screen had been pushed aside again. Hallie chuckled and pulled out her phone.

"Put the phone away." The voice behind her was cold. And familiar.

Malcolm.

Her heart jumped into her throat. She forced herself to breathe. Slowly turned around.

"Hello, Hallie." Malcolm's smile sent chills down her spine. "I've missed you."

She swallowed, took a step back.

He matched her step and that's when she saw the knife. He waved it in her face, eyes cold.

"Scream and I'll take pleasure in using it. I've killed before. I know exactly where to cut."

She believed him.

"You're lovely. Like I remember." His eyes bored into her. "So young."

Hallie couldn't move.

"Call me Dave if you want to." His nails bit into her arms as he forced her hands behind her back and tied them. She struggled, and the point of the knife dug into her back.

"Stay still or I'll kill you. I mean it."

His menacing tone left her sure he meant every word.

He spoke close to her mouth. "It's time we got to know each other."

She turned her face.

His mouth moved closer and she could feel his breath on her lips. "You love me, remember?" He stepped back and his eyes moved from her hair down to her socked feet. He smiled in approval.

"No shoes. Makes it harder to run."

God, help me! Please!

She wasn't sure if Malcolm was psychotic or purely evil, but the fear she felt now was the same fear she'd felt when the island man's rough hands had tightened around her neck, choking her.

Oh God, what do I do now?

A knock came at the door. Mac must have seen Malcolm.

Malcolm waved the knife in her face. "Tell them you're busy. Or I …" He pointed the knife at her neck. His order was low and fierce. What should she do? God had clearly sent help, but she didn't want anyone getting hurt on her behalf. Should she make a run for it?

She looked at the door handle. Her hands were still tied.

Malcolm pushed her forward until she stood a few inches from the door. He turned the handle and in the same move slipped out of view behind the door. He remained hidden, but he was right beside her. Poised, knife ready. One swish of that knife and he'd slice her neck.

The door swung slowly open.

Josh.

He stood looking at her, that beloved cheeky grin on his face, and Bandit in his arms. Hallie blinked. She couldn't risk his life. Couldn't risk him getting hurt. As much as she wanted to throw herself into his familiar embrace and cling to him, she wouldn't. Couldn't. The ties on her hands were tight.

"Missing someone?" Josh grinned, his blue eyes sparkling.

Hallie nodded. "She got out."

Josh stepped back teasingly. "Hey, I meant me."

Hallie felt dazed. "You can put her down." Her voice came out tight and strained.

Josh looked surprised and hurt, but he seemed to pull

himself together. "You have to at least ask me in for a drink. I've come all this way to bring back your poor, lost kitten."

What should she do? Josh was clearly in the mood for games, but it was too dangerous. She had to do whatever it took to send him away. She would rather die than see Josh hurt. The thought shook her. What a time to realize just how deeply she loved him.

Just as she was about to die.

———

"You better go, Josh." Hallie's voice was cold and she looked away, but not before Josh saw the desperate, frightened look in her eyes. She was hiding her hands behind her back. Something was wrong. Way wrong.

"What? You don't want the kitten anymore?" he asked, biding his time.

"No. You have her." She glanced quickly around. Now Josh knew something was wrong. Without waiting for an invite that clearly wasn't coming, he stepped inside.

A man came into view. He put his arm around Hallie, and she froze.

Josh searched her eyes. "Everything all right, Hallie?"

The stranger, an older, gray-haired man gave Josh a cold look. "She wants you to leave. We're busy."

"Go, Josh." Hallie's voice came out in a whisper, her eyes pleading and frightened.

Josh ignored her and held out a hand to the man. "I don't think we've met."

"No." The man's tone was hard.

Josh stood to his full height. "Who are you?"

"Josh ..." Hallie's voice pleaded with him to stop.

The man stepped closer to Josh in a threatening way. "I'm Hallie's fiancé."

Josh's stomach dropped. Then fear crept through him. None of this was right in any sense of the word.

"And we'd like some time together. Alone." He looked at Hallie and gave a leering smile that made Josh feel sick. His eyes went to the man's arm so inappropriately around Holly. The stranger's fingers dug into her side in a forceful, controlling way, and Josh saw red.

Before he knew what he was doing, he flew at the man, throwing him off balance and to the ground. Josh fell on top of him, and a knife clattered to the floor. The impact had knocked the breath out of both of them. They began to wrestle, and Hallie screamed.

"Watch out, Josh," Hallie shouted.

Josh threw his head to the side just before the stranger's fist could slam into him.

"Holly, call 911." Josh struggled to hold the man still, gulping in breaths of air.

"I can't."

Josh didn't have time to question her. The man was throwing wild punches and wrestling against his hold. Pain hit him as a punch landed on the side of his face. His ear burned. Stunned, he pulled back. The man struggled free from Josh's grasp, and ran from the house.

Josh was still getting his bearings, wiping a trickle of blood from his ear when Mac burst in. Josh tried to catch his breath, tried to control his fury. "Call 911."

"I have."

Josh closed his eyes. *Thank you, Lord!*

He turned to see Hallie on her knees on the floor, rocking backwards and forwards, hands tied behind her back.

"Hallie?" That man would pay for this. He tried to tamp down his anger. He needed to help Hallie. She needed gentleness. Mac took a knife from the drying rack and cut the ties on her wrists. Her hands immediately went to cover her face. Josh dropped to the floor beside her. She was shaking like a leaf. He put his arms around her, surprised when she broke into rasping sobs.

"I thought he was going to kill you, Josh. I thought I'd never see you again."

He moved her hands from her face and lifted her to a standing position.

"Hey, Hallie, it's okay. I'm okay. It's you I was worried about." His head pounded and his vision swam. *Please God, don't let me get a migraine. Not now.*

His vision cleared.

Hallie stared at him, tears streaming down her cheeks. Then she reached a shaking hand to his ear. "Oh Josh, you're bleeding."

He gave a lopsided grin. "It's only a flesh wound."

She laughed somewhat hysterically and threw her arms around him, burying her head in his neck. It felt good having her there. She was the perfect height. This adult Hallie fit better into his arms than the little girl had. She belonged here. In his arms.

———

HALLIE TRIED to concentrate on what the sheriff was saying, but all she wanted to do was enjoy the feel of Josh's arms around her. His touch was the extreme opposite of Malcolm's. How could she go from feeling terrified to safe and protected in such a short space of time?

Sheriff Thompson drew her attention back. "My men caught him hiding like a coward in a garden down the street, but we need a statement from you. Are you up to coming down to the station?"

Hallie nodded.

"Your young man can come with you—we need his statement as well."

Hallie's eyes flew to Josh's at the sheriff's assumption. Josh winked at her.

They drove in silence to the station. Josh sat close beside her in the back seat. His presence was comforting and secure. His strength and maturity in the face of danger had revealed he was a man she could trust with her life. She didn't know what to do with that knowledge.

They arrived at the station at the same time as Malcolm was escorted, handcuffed, into another room. He glanced coldly at Hallie and nausea swirled in her stomach.

The sheriff touched her shoulder. "Don't worry. He can't get to you. He's not likely to ever get out of prison."

Josh glanced from Malcolm to Hallie, looking troubled. "Who is he?"

"Malcolm Cleary, but he has several aliases," the sheriff said. "He's a pedophile out on parole. We've been trying to track him down since he met with Hallie in Springfield. He's since tried to abduct a fifteen-year-old girl in Utah and force her to marry him."

Josh jerked back. "So he was going to abduct Holly and force her to marry him?" He looked at Hallie. "Is he the internet friend you told me about? The reason you left?"

Hallie nodded, her gaze skirting away from his.

"Josh, you go to that room." The sheriff pointed down the hall. "Hallie, you come with me."

Hallie felt Josh looking at her, but she still couldn't meet his eyes.

"Why didn't you confide in me?" she heard him ask as she moved toward the other interview room. "Am I really so untrustworthy?"

He sounded so sad. Regret tightened its jagged edges around

her heart, and she couldn't speak. If she'd trusted Josh, been more open with everyone, all of this might have been prevented. What was it that made her continue to hold back from everyone?

ONCE THE STATEMENTS WERE SIGNED, Sheriff Thomson drove them back to Hallie's cottage. Hallie rolled tense shoulders, her heart hurting. She should feel relieved it was over, but Josh was uncharacteristically silent, his expression unreadable.

Once inside the cottage, she felt his eyes on her. She closed and locked the door behind them. Her hands still shook. She drew in a deep breath and turned to face Josh, to try to explain.

"I internet dated him for two years." Her voice shook and it all came rushing out. "He told me he was a Christian surfer named Dave. I thought he loved me, even thought he might be the one God had for me. I told him everything about me. Everything. Then he came to meet me in person ..." Her chin quivered. "I escaped him, but my dreams were shattered. The police said I'd be safer to get away."

"You never told me."

A tear squeezed out and rolled down her cheek. "I didn't tell anyone. I felt so stupid."

He kept looking at her, that wounded expression on his face. The evidence of the pain she had caused. Unable to help herself, she flew into his arms, and her face crumpled. "I'm so sorry, Josh." Cries welled up from somewhere deep inside, a well of hurt she hadn't allowed herself to feel in years.

Josh froze as she clung to him.

"You're right," she said through broken sobs. "I don't trust anyone. I don't know how to love, how to show affection. I've never kissed anyone in my life. Not even a cheek peck. What is wrong with me?"

She cried harder, all the control of her childhood years completely broken.

"Hey, Holly," Josh sounded worried. His arms came around her, holding her tentatively at first, then more firmly. "It's okay. It's okay." One of his hands smoothed her hair and the other ran up and down her back, comforting and reassuring.

She tried to control herself, while Josh held her and let her cry. Finally she pulled back, taking deep, gulping breaths.

Humiliation washed over her at her display of uncontrolled emotion. "Sorry."

"What for?" Josh's smile was gentle. Tender.

"For being so ... such a mess."

He reached up and wiped one of her tears. "It happens to all of us sometimes, Holly. I began to think it must never happen to you, but I figured you were just keeping it all to yourself. Trying to handle things on your own. But God gave us each other for a reason."

Each other? Did he mean that? Her eyes must have shown her uncertainty and hope.

He smiled. "I know that God made us for relationship with Him first and foremost, but humans need humans too, sweetheart. And I need you."

"You do?"

He nodded and reached for her hand, eyes intently watching her. "Do you think you could learn to trust me?"

Her heart broke at his question, at the hope and doubt warring in his eyes. "I do trust you."

"Really?" His expression was both challenging and gentle. His eyes never left hers as he trailed a finger down her cheek then slowly, deliberately, ran his thumb over her lower lip.

Her heart pounded and panic battled with desire she'd never experienced before. "Josh, I've never ..."

His look was full of understanding. "Will you trust me?" His voice was soft and deep.

She drew in a breath and nodded. When he looked at her that way, she would trust him with anything.

He came closer, then his mouth stopped inches from hers. His eyes locked on hers, breath tickling her lips. "Just so you know, this is a first for me, too. The first time I've so badly wanted to kiss someone … the first time I've been scared to in case I mess it up, in case I ruin something, hurt someone precious."

Heat filled her chest and anticipation thrummed in her veins at the desire she saw in his eyes. She'd never wanted so badly to be kissed. All fear was replaced by a burning need of him.

He tilted his head and spoke with his lips brushing against hers, tantalizing, drawing out the moment, increasing her longing. "Before I kiss you the way I'm desperate to, I need to know … Do you think you can ever respect me? As an equal?"

Her hands came up to tenderly hold either side of his face. The bristles on his cheeks grazed her fingers.

"Definitely."

He searched her eyes. "I love you, Holly," he whispered. Then finally his lips claimed hers. Gentle yet firm as they moved against hers, safe yet so dangerously sensual. Overwhelming joy filled her. Josh Ladan was loving her with a much deeper, mature, complete love than the boy Josh ever knew how to give.

She wanted more. More of this feeling unlike any she'd ever experienced. More of his tenderness, his desire, his love. He sensed her need and deepened his kiss, pulling her tight against him until her senses swam and she needed to breathe, to gain control of herself and her body.

She pulled back.

His eyes held the same expression of wonder she was feeling.

Then he smiled a warm, slow smile and tears leaked out between her lashes.

"I love you, Josh," she whispered. "God knew how much I needed you. That's why he brought me back to Trinity Lakes. I've never loved someone like I love you."

"Oh Holly." His fingers stroked the back of her neck. "I want to be with you always. I want us to be a team. I want to share your amazing dreams, your inspirational vision to see children come to know Christ. And I want you to share my dreams, too."

She smiled through her tears. "I want that too. More than anything. I love you more than I thought I could love anyone. I can't imagine my life without you."

He smiled at her. Not a slow, lazy smile, but a complete, pure expression of the joy in his heart.

"Same goes, Holly," he whispered.

There was no teasing in his blue eyes. Just a depth and intensity she'd never dreamed she'd see there. He brought his lips to hers again in another soul-stirring kiss.

She'd never thought she could feel this way. There was no reason. No analyzing, no intelligent thought. Just feelings. Deep. Strong. There were no words to explain it. Except maybe one.

Love.

CHAPTER TWENTY-SIX

Josh insisted Hallie come back and stay in Esther's room that night. There was no way he was leaving her alone.

He'd called Mom from the police station, and the whole family swarmed on them as they came in the front door.

When they'd been thoroughly hugged, Josh led Hallie to the living room, his arm around her waist. Jodie gave him a questioning look and he smiled. Let her think what she liked.

Hallie appeared shy as everyone's eyes turned to her, waiting to hear the story. Jodie gasped throughout the telling, looking as though she wanted to tear Malcolm to shreds. Josh shared the sentiment.

"You definitely need to stay here tonight," Mom said decisively after giving Hallie yet another hug. "There's no way I could sleep knowing you're on your own in that little cottage ."

Josh's mouth tipped. He felt the same way. Hallie looked exhausted.

"Can I get you a drink? Something to eat?" he asked.

She smiled an exclusive smile at him, and his heart melted. "I wouldn't mind a hot chocolate."

Reluctantly, he removed his arm from her waist and went to

the kitchen. Jodie followed him. "What's going on?" she whispered.

Josh pretended not to know what she was talking about. "She's a bit shaken, obviously."

"No," Jodie rolled her eyes. "I'm talking about the adoration in her eyes whenever she looks at you. I'm talking about your tenderness when you look at her, when you touch her."

Josh pulled a mug down from the cupboard. "Sounds to me like you're telling the story. You tell me what's going on."

"You're in love with her."

Josh smiled. "Yeah. Have been since we were kids, really. It just took a while to find the real Hallie again."

Jodie shook her head. "Well, miracles happen after all."

"Hey! Loving me is not a miracle."

She smiled. "No, but you being brave enough to admit you love her is."

He couldn't argue with that.

Josh took Hallie home the following morning. She looked nervously down the street as she unlocked the front door of the cottage. When she was settled in the sofa, he sat beside her. She shot him a startled look, obviously expecting him to sit opposite. But then she smiled.

He crossed his leg over his knee and took her hand in his. "I have an idea. I'm hoping you'll hear me out and not say no."

She looked at him out of those big blue eyes, hesitant and unsure. He prayed for courage.

"I want you to move back in with Mom and Dad. I want to take over your lease here."

She blinked and he could see her processing it. Then she tilted her head. "Why?"

"One, it's safer for you. And two, I want to challenge myself. Learn what it's like to fend for myself. I'm almost twenty-four years old, and I think it's high time I had a go at it."

She bit her lip. "What about your migraines?"

"They're not life threatening. I'll be okay."

Her eyes teared up. "I don't like thinking of you alone and in pain."

"I promise I'll call you if I get a migraine. But maybe I'm cured. I didn't end up with one after Malcolm hit me."

Still she didn't look convinced. "Why don't you move into the Bible college accommodation?"

He shook his head. "Been there, done that."

That's right. He'd lived there with his parents as a child.

He grinned. "Besides, this cottage has grown on me."

She chewed her lip, then began to smile. "Are you sure?"

He drew her closer against his side. "Never been more sure of anything in my life."

"I guess I could come and help you with your laundry and cleaning if you need it. Teach you how it's done." Her teasing smile lit her face.

He dropped his mouth open in mock offence, then nudged her with his shoulder. "Actually, if I play on being a poor, disabled bachelor, you'll have to visit me"

She laughed. He liked her laugh.

"I did hope you could help me with study, though. I will need help, even with accommodations and all, but perhaps you'd be willing to help me with reading and writing."

Her eyes glistened. "I'd love to."

He pictured her sitting beside him, reading to him in that clear, lilting voice of hers and smiled. This was the warm, generous Hallie he'd always known and loved.

A loud honking sounded from next door and Hallie smiled. "Will Mac's geese bother you?"

Bandit jumped up and curled into his lap. "Not at all." He

stroked the cat's fur. "And being next to the Junk—Mac means Brandon can visit us both at once."

Hallie's look turned thoughtful. "You know, I don't think Brandon dislikes Jodie as much as he pretends to."

He smiled. "I thought the same thing. And vice versa."

Her eyes lit and a satisfied smile filled her lips.

He laughed. "Are you matchmaking?"

"I don't need to. God's good at that. I mean, look at us." Her smile turned downright smug. He laughed then looked down at Bandit, who was now purring noisily in his lap. He tickled her under the chin.

Hallie stroked her fur. "My cat fell in love with you before I did."

Josh captured her eyes with his own. "You weren't in love with me when we were kids?"

She blushed prettily and looked away. "I probably was. But these feelings, this love … it's so much more."

"Same."

She looked back and met his gaze. "It didn't even occur to me that someone like you could love me this way," she whispered.

Josh ran his thumb over her fingers. "Why? Because I'm too immature to value your good points?"

Hallie laughed. "No."

"Then why?"

"Because you're too … Well, you know."

He grinned. "Good-looking and desirable?"

She let out an honest to goodness giggle. "Something like that."

"Modest, too."

"Exactly."

Josh laughed and ran his knuckles down her cheek. "You're good for my ego, Holly. You keep me grounded. And I want you to keep me accountable."

She looked uncertain. "In what way?"

"I don't want to lose direction in my life again. I want to keep the passion to care for God's people. I don't want to get carried away with preserving my own happiness and comfort. I want to put God first, always. Whatever the cost."

When Hallie didn't respond, he looked more closely at her. "What's wrong?"

She didn't answer and Josh could tell a wrestle was going on in her heart and mind.

———

HALLIE DIDN'T KNOW how to explain what she was feeling. Something about Josh's desire to put God first bothered her. She knew it was time to face up to her deepest feelings.

Her parents had always put God first and she had felt insignificant. She had been jealous of her parents' devotion to God and the way they left her to grow up so quickly, alone. She had resented being considered a genius due to finishing her homeschooling so early. She'd been hurt when her parents rejoiced at her early completion, because that meant they could travel overseas without the concern of her education or financial well-being. Her parents didn't have time for children. Didn't have room for her in their lives or hearts.

Hallie looked directly into Josh's blue eyes. The concern and tenderness she read there warmed her heart. She could trust him with her deepest thoughts. Her fears.

"Josh, when you find what God has for you, I hope you always remember the children."

His expression softened and he ran gentle fingers up and down her arm. "Oh Holly, you've been so hurt."

She blinked back tears.

He pulled her hand over into his lap and gently stroked the back of her fingers. "If I'm like Jesus, I'll never forget the children. Jesus had a special place in his ministry for them. Others didn't bother, but He made time for them."

"My parents never did."

Josh acknowledged the truth of that with a nod. "Perhaps your parents weren't gifted with children. But I know they loved and admired you. I could see it in their eyes."

Hallie's eyes filled with tears. "I didn't want to be admired. I wanted to be a child. I wanted to feel free to make mistakes and know someone would be there to catch me, to help me and still love me. I wanted to be able to curl up in my father's arms and know I was important to him. That I was loved. Was it too much to ask?"

He drew her closer, pressed a kiss against her brow. "You'll always be God's child, Holly. He was a parent to you, wasn't He? He filled in the gaps your parents left because of their devotion to Him. He gave you my family when you needed one so badly. Only you didn't know how to open up to us and trust us."

Hallie stared at him. Got caught in his eyes. He spoke with wisdom and discernment. He was right.

Shyly, she reached a hand and touched his ear, still red, but healing from Malcolm's fist.

"I need you to keep me accountable too," she said. "Make sure I'm open and honest. And make sure I always remember that in teaching those kids, I'm preparing God's dearly loved children for His Kingdom."

Josh nodded as he pulled her into his lap and wrapped his arms around her. "I feel like I'm finally getting to know the real Hallie Hollaway." He touched his lips to hers. "And the more I get to know her, the more I love her."

She snuggled into his chest and smiled as she looked up at him. She'd thought she was running from Malcolm when really, God had been teaching her to trust Him. And leading her into Josh's arms. She'd never known such love before.

· · ·

Hallie leaned over the fence, telling Mac she'd be moving out after Christmas and Josh would be moving in. She stopped mid-sentence when an unfamiliar car drove up her driveway. She stiffened. Her heart set up a crazy pounding. Memories flashed and she stared at the vehicle.

Mac came closer and followed her gaze.

"I'm here, Hallie," he said. "That's what friends are for."

She smiled, eyes still fixed on the car as she made herself relax. "Thanks, Mac."

It couldn't be Malcolm, so why did she keep thinking he'd turn up at her door again? Slowly she pushed off the fence and headed down the driveway. The driver and passenger doors opened in unison, and Hallie let out a gasp.

"Mom. Dad. What are you doing here?"

They both looked awkward as they studied her. Hallie shook her head. This was ridiculous. They weren't affectionate people, but everything in her wanted to hug them and she would.

She hugged Mom first, and then Dad. Dad stood stiffly as though he didn't know what to do. Hallie grinned at them.

"Come inside. See my little cottage. Oh, it's good to see you."

"It's a nice cottage," Mom said, sitting down on the sofa. Dad sat beside her.

Hallie sat, too. "You haven't told me what you're doing here."

Dad cleared his throat. "We needed to see for ourselves that you're all right. The Ladans told us what happened with that disgusting man."

Hallie frowned in confusion. "But I thought you were overseas."

"We were."

Truth slowly dawned on Hallie. "You came all this way to see if I was okay? You flew all this way just to see me?"

Both parents nodded and the controlled, reserved daughter they had known for so many years disappeared as Halie beamed at them with unbridled joy.

"Oh Mom, Dad, I don't know what to say. Except thank you!"

Her parents stared at her in shock, and she wanted to laugh. Poor Mom and Dad weren't used to her spontaneous expression. They didn't know everything that had happened while they were away. Love was a healing thing. God was a God of healing.

Hallie showed her parents around her little cottage. She introduced them to Mac, and went with them to visit the Ladans.

Josh drew her into the kitchen as their parents caught up in the living room. He reached for both her hands and smiled into her eyes. "This is unexpected."

"I can't believe it, Josh." Hallie's cheeks hurt from smiling. "They came all the way across the ocean, left their ministry, to see if I was okay."

He laughed. "Told you they loved you. How could they not?"

"Oh, you." She wondered if she'd ever stop blushing when he complimented her.

"Actually, I'm glad they're here." He lifted one of her hands and held it over his heart. She felt its rapid beating. "I know we need to take things slow, Hallie." His voice was deep and serious. "I need to find my feet as a bachelor living on his own and going to Bible college, and you need to be sure of the man I am. We both need to seek God, find a rhythm as a couple. But I want to tell your dad my intentions. Ask him if I can court you."

Hallie laughed. "That's a bit old-fashioned, isn't it?"

"Maybe, but maybe I'm just an old-fashioned kind of guy."

She giggled.

"Holly, did you just giggle? The Holly I know doesn't giggle. She's way too mature for that."

She wanted to laugh, but she couldn't. It stuck in her throat, and she swallowed down a lump. How could she not have seen

Josh for who he really was? How could she have judged him so harshly? The love she felt for him was overwhelming.

She tugged on his shirt and drew him closer until their lips met. She felt his sharp intake of breath. "Oh Holly."

Then he kissed her like she was longing to be kissed. She got lost in the intense awareness of him, the sense of belonging, the overwhelming feelings that were oh, so right. If this was any indication of courting Josh Ladan style, she looked forward to every moment. It wouldn't be boring, that was for sure.

EPILOGUE

Hallie and Josh walked along the edge of the lake. She lifted her face to the sun, enjoying its warmth, enjoying God's fatherly delight shining on her. Winter was over, and spring was here. Three months of courting had changed her deep inside. She hadn't known how it would feel to be so special to someone, to be the most important person in their world. Love had to be one of the most healing things on earth. Through Josh, she now understood more of God's love.

She looked out across the lake, the water shimmering beneath the spring sunshine, wildflowers beginning to bloom. A brood of ducklings waddled along the lake's edge behind their mother. The mother dove in and the ducklings hesitated.

Come on, little ones. Take the plunge. She wouldn't take you there if it wasn't safe.

Their mother called. One by one, they cautiously entered the water and Hallie smiled.

"There's Mac." She pointed to where Mac stood a little further up, looking out on the water, shading his eyes. She didn't know if she'd ever get used to seeing him without his beard.

"He said he was going to release one of his birds this morning," Josh said. "Looks like it went well."

"Oh, I love it when he can release them back into the wild." Hallie danced in front of him. "Rhonda Ingalls said she reckons he's released over three hundred birds in the last twenty years. She said he's been nominated for some special award for his work with wildlife and the environment."

Josh laughed at her excited chattering. "You know you should never listen to what Rhonda Ingalls says."

Hallie giggled. "Rhonda looked so excited when she caught us putting those groceries on Mrs. Carrigan's porch." She giggled again. "It was like she won the lottery. You know everyone in town will know it's you?"

"Hey." He shook his head and gave a lopsided grin. "We're a team now. Whatever scandal I'm involved in, you are too."

She laughed merrily. "Hardly a scandal, Josh. The scandal is that even though you're a bachelor living in Frog Swamp, you keep your house tidy and even buy toothbrushes for my cat."

He tilted his head and drew her to a stop, pulling her into his arms. "Maybe I see Bandit as my cat now."

"What?" she pretended horror. "You would take back the gift you gave me and break my little-girl heart?"

"I could replace your cat with a Barbie if you like."

She screwed up her nose, poking him in the chest. "You and I both know that's no compensation."

He pushed her finger away, eyes twinkling then locked his hands behind her back. "Would this be suitable compensation?"

She smiled as his lips met hers in a tender, passionate kiss.

When he pulled back, his eyes were serious. "Hallie, since we're not having any secrets between us, I need to confess something to you."

Her heart sank. *God, help me be understanding.*

He drew in a deep breath and couldn't seem to meet her eyes.

"That check the church sent to you …"

She blinked.

He took her hands, wound his fingers around hers. Then met her eyes. "It was my idea that we ask people to donate. I got Dad to arrange it."

She tried to process his words.

He rushed on. "I don't know if it was God's prompting or the fact that deep down I so desperately wanted you to stay, but I wasn't trying to manipulate you. I want you to know that."

She couldn't let him finish. She threw her arms around his neck and held him tight as tears squeezed from between her eyelids and down her cheeks.

"Oh Josh, I was so, so blind. So judgmental. How could I not see it?"

He laughed, loosening her arms around his neck. "It helps if you have all the information, which you didn't. And I was equally as blind, thinking my life was over because the path to my dreams got a bit rougher."

"But they weren't just dreams. They were God's plans."

He nodded. "I do think He wants me to be a pastor, but after Bible college … well, how would you feel if He called me back to stacking supermarket shelves? To passing on old stock to those in need? Would it fit in with your dreams?"

She tipped her head back and looked deep into his eyes. "All I ever wanted was for you to know and love God. You, Josh Ladan, are more than I ever hoped or dreamed." She didn't try to hold back her tears. "If God tells you to stack supermarket shelves, there's no way I'm going to say you should be striving for full-time ministry in your own strength. If he tells you to collect trash for cash, I won't stand in your way. Some of the most caring, admirable people I know are humble servants. Like Jesus."

Josh cleared his throat. Blinked. Nodded. He wiped her tears with his thumbs. His eyes glistened and she bit her lip as she stared up at the man she loved more than any other in the world.

"Life sure doesn't turn out the way we expect, does it?" she said.

He drew in a deep breath and his mouth tipped in one corner. "Well, I don't know about that. I think that deep down I always knew I would one day marry a girl with red hair and freckles. Ever since I met one who stole my heart."

Her heart stuttered, warmed by the tender look he was giving her. She searched his eyes. He didn't look like he was teasing. His gaze never left hers. Then he dropped to one knee, pulled a box from his pocket, and opened it. Her eyes took in a delicate diamond ring. She swallowed hard, trying to process what she was seeing; what he was doing.

"Will you marry me, Hallie Hollaway?" His lips took on a small, hopeful smile. "Will you share your cat with me?"

She choked on a laugh.

He drew in a deep breath. "And will you give me the privilege of supporting you in the ministry God has given you all the days of your life, and will you honor me by supporting me in whatever God calls me to? Will you keep me accountable? Remind me of the love of Jesus for me and for His children?" His smile turned sheepish. "And for our own children someday?"

"Oh, Josh." Hallie couldn't finish. Her tears came faster. She threw herself into his arms.

"Hey, the ring," he said, but his words were muffled by her lips on his.

His arms came around her waist and she heard the ring drop to the ground. They'd worry about picking it up later.

Nobody looked surprised when Josh led Hallie into the Ladans' living room and announced their good news.

"Show me the ring." Jodie glared at her brother, and he grinned back at her. "Josh wouldn't show me before he gave it to you."

Hallie held out her hand while Jodie inspected the ring.

"It's not the ring she cares about," Josh said. "She almost threw it in the lake."

"I did not." Hallie laughed, playfully swiping at him with her ring-bearing hand. Jodie snatched it back and took a closer look.

Josh winked at Hallie. The truth of how the ring had fallen out of the box into the grass and how they'd taken a good twenty minutes to find it because they kept stopping for another kiss would stay between the two of them. Maybe they'd share it with their children someday.

Everyone laughed and hugged and congratulated them.

"You really are family now," Aunty Lil said. "In every way."

Hallie tried to hold back the tears of gratefulness that stung her eyes. Josh met her gaze and smiled. A slow, understanding smile that expressed love like she'd never known.

"I love you," she mouthed as a tear escaped.

"Love you too." He came up beside her, licked a finger and wiped away a tear.

She grabbed his finger. "Hey!"

His eyes widened in pretend innocence. "There was something there."

Of all the cheeky …

He grinned at her. "Now we're even."

"Oh no," she whispered back. "It's only just started."

He laughed then drew her closer. "You know, I once heard it said that no man can kiss the woman he loves with his hands in his pockets and a silly grin on his face."

A small smile curved her lips. "Is that so?"

Her breath caught at the look in his eyes. He gently touched the side of her mouth and she found herself lost in his gaze.

Then both his hands slid through her hair before he proved the truth of the claim with a passionate kiss.

The End
Read the next Trinity Lakes Romance,
No Matter How Far

A NOTE FROM THE AUTHOR

Thank you for reading *Where Our Hearts Lie*, the sixth book in the Trinity Lakes series. I hope you enjoyed sharing Josh and Hallie's journey as much as I enjoyed writing it.

I usually write Young Adult Christian Fiction, so writing Christian Romance was a new experience. It's also the first time I've written in a multi-author series. It's been a great adventure.

Please be sure to check out the other books in the Trinity Lakes series:

1. *Never Find Another You* by Narelle Atkins
2. *The Ocean Between Us* by Meredith Resce
3. *I'll Always Choose You* by Lisa Renee
4. *Always By My Side* by Iola Goulton
5. *Love Somebody Like You* by Carolyn Miller
6. **Where Our Hearts Lie** by Jenny Glazebrook
7. *No Matter How Far* by Sara Beth Williams.

You can purchase them here: Trinity Lakes Romance

If you enjoyed Where Our Hearts Lie, please check out my website to find out more about me and my writing. www.jennyglazebrook.com

You can also pre-order my second book in the Trinity Lakes series, *In Truth and Love*, due for release 30th April, 2024.

***

Reviews help other readers find new-to-them authors, so I'd really appreciate it if you can spare a moment to write a quick review at Goodreads or your place of purchase.

MORE BOOKS FROM JENNY GLAZEBROOK

If you enjoy horse stories with a twist, you might enjoy my Aussie Sky Series which includes six novels about a lovable ex-circus family, their relationship with God and the lives they touch:

Blaze in the Storm
Heart of Thunder
Clouds of Prayer
Mist of the Morning
Clinging to Rainbows
Forgiving Sky

If you enjoy contemporary inspirational stories about new and young adults learning what it means to walk with God in a broken world, check out my Bateman Family novels published by Daughters of Love and Light (DOLL Ministries). These can be found through my publisher and other book retailers.

https://dollministries.com/product-category/the-bateman-family-novels/

I love to hear from my readers, so please feel free to email me: jenny@jennyglazebrook.com

ACKNOWLEDGMENTS

As always it takes a team to write a book and I want to acknowledge all those whose valuable input has made this story what it is.

To my fellow Trinity Lakes authors, Narelle Atkins, Meredith Resce, Lisa Renee, Iola Goulton, Carolyn Miller and Sara Beth Williams, your support in this process has been invaluable. A special thanks to Carolyn for walking me through each step of the way. I couldn't have done it without you.

Thank you also to Heather Pine and Heather Hood Lucero who helped me with US culture and language differences and gave valuable feedback to improve my story. I learned a lot. Any mistakes are my own.

Thank you to my children, Merridy, Clarity and Micah who proofread my original draft for me. Amy, I look forward to having you join the team when you're older.

And as always, thank you to my husband, Rob. I love that you take the time to go over the many versions of my manuscripts, to pick up inconsistencies and encourage me. What would I do without your logical mind? I love sharing this journey of life with you.

Above all thank you Father God for your love, inspiration, and the gift of creativity you have given me. It's a joy to write these stories with you.

ABOUT THE AUTHOR

Jenny Glazebrook lives in a small country town in Australia. She and her husband Rob have four children and many rescue animals who fill their lives with joy.

Jenny writes stories which capture what it means to know Jesus and live for him in a broken world.

She has a Diploma of Theology, is a qualified chaplain and experienced inspirational speaker. She loves to encourage others to understand God's love, see His hand in their lives, and walk with Him each day.

ALSO BY JENNY GLAZEBROOK

The Aussie Sky Series (YA fiction):

Blaze in the Storm

Heart of Thunder

Clouds of Prayer

Mist of the Morning

Clinging to Rainbows

Forgiving Sky

The Bateman Family Novels (YA/new adult fiction):

Daring Clare

Saving Beth

Framing Fleur

Seeing Jess

Living Melody

Loving Zoe (coming soon)

Coming soon:

Molly the Dog-Sheep and Other True Pet Parables

Collaborative works:

Wellspring Devotional Journal

Dear Jesus Diaries

starts, second chances, and romance abounds. You'll meet cowboys and swoony bachelors, sweet and sassy ladies, and your new best friends. This series of sweet and clean standalone Christian romances will warm your heart, inspire your faith, and bring a smile to your soul.

Check out the other books in the Trinity Lakes series:

Never Find Another You - Narelle Atkins

The Ocean Between Us - Meredith Resce

I'll Always Choose You - Lisa Renee

Always By My Side - Iola Goulton

Love Somebody Like You - Carolyn Miller

Where Our Hearts Lie - Jenny Glazebrook

No Matter How Far - Sara Beth Williams

Over the Rainbow - Meredith Resce

Tangled Up in Love - Carolyn Miller

In Truth and Love - Jenny Glazebrook